The guy gave a whole new meaning to the term hardened *soldier.*

"Oh, my," Ivy murmured in appreciation, devouring Garrett with her eyes. He was like hot silk in her hand. In awe, she smoothed a thumb across the head of his erection. When it came away slick with moisture, an answering heat pooled in her center. Unable to resist, she circled her fingers around him.

He jerked reflexively in her hand and made a deep sound of pleasure. When she glanced at him again, the expression in his eyes—hot and intense—consumed her, made her want to see just how far she could go before he completely lost control.

"I don't know, soldier," she mused aloud, sending him a sultry look. "Your situation appears...dire."

He smiled, but Ivy didn't miss how his muscles tightened as she squeezed him gently. "Yeah," he said, his voice husky. "But don't worry, sweetheart. The word *retreat* isn't in my vocabulary...."

Blaze™

Dear Reader,

I'll admit it—I'm a movie junkie! There's something about getting pulled into a really great flick that just makes you forget everything else. But sometimes I can't help wondering what it's like for the actors, what they do when they're required to shoot a love scene with an entire film crew watching. How do they "become" the characters they portray? Does the line between make-believe and reality ever get blurred? As a writer, I couldn't help but see the possibilities....

Aspiring actress Ivy James is thrilled to be cast opposite Hollywood's latest golden boy in a military adventure that's packed with romance. But when the real-life hero shows up on the set as a technical consultant, Ivy's acting skills take a vacation. How can she concentrate on the love scenes with special ops soldier Garrett Stokes watching her every move? She can't. But when he offers to coach her through the scenes, sparks fly, both on-screen and off!

I hope you enjoy reading their story!

Hugs,

Karen Foley

OVERNIGHT SENSATION
Karen Foley

HARLEQUIN®

TORONTO • NEW YORK • LONDON
AMSTERDAM • PARIS • SYDNEY • HAMBURG
STOCKHOLM • ATHENS • TOKYO • MILAN • MADRID
PRAGUE • WARSAW • BUDAPEST • AUCKLAND

ISBN-13: 978-0-373-79426-3
ISBN-10:   0-373-79426-6

OVERNIGHT SENSATION

ABOUT THE AUTHOR

Karen Foley is an incurable romantic. When she's not working for the Department of Defense, she loves writing sexy romances with strong military heroes and happy endings. She lives in Massachusetts with her husband and two daughters, and enjoys hearing from her readers. You can find out more about her by visiting www.karenefoley.com.

Books by Karen Foley
HARLEQUIN BLAZE
353—FLYBOY

This book is dedicated to some of the amazing women in my life. To Samantha Hunter, who came up with the great title for this book; to Barbara, Cathryn, Denise, Michelle and Nina, for providing constant support; to Vicki and Ellen for playing the name game; and to my mother, Mary Jo, a true role model and inspiration.

1

NO DOUBT ABOUT IT—she was going to die. She could almost see the headlines: B-List Actress Killed In Chicken Bus Accident. Dreams Of Hitting The Big Time Crushed With Her.

For someone who'd just been chosen to star opposite Hollywood's hottest actor, Ivy James sure didn't feel like red-carpet material. While she certainly hadn't expected mobs of eager fans to greet her, or a stretch limousine to sit waiting to whisk her away to a five-star hotel, still she'd held out hope that someone—even a minor crew member—would come to meet her flight. But no one had been waiting for her at the arrivals terminal, and in the end, her only option had been to stick with the itinerary provided to her and hop a public bus for the eighty-mile ride from the resort city of Veracruz to the remote mountain town of Pancho Viejo. And now here she was, bone-tired, sweaty and, above all, scared stiff, on a suicide ride through the Mexican jungle.

The garishly painted bus, decked out with a roof rack and brush guards, lurched violently to one side of the badly potholed road, throwing her against her neighbor. The driver—or *piloto,* as he'd called himself—apparently believed that although his vehicle might look like a beat-up school bus, it was in fact a finely tuned Formula One race car.

For the past hour they'd careened along steep mountain roads. Twice, they'd passed other buses on blind, hairpin curves. Ivy had squeezed her eyes shut, but the honking horns, smoking brakes and violent rocking weren't things she'd soon forget.

With a muttered apology to her neighbor, Ivy clutched her overnight bag tighter on her lap and pressed herself against the window, praying she didn't throw up. She cast a sideways glance at the old woman beside her. Her brown face was seamed with creases, her eyes were closed and her mouth worked soundlessly as her callused fingers slid over the beads of a rosary. The sight gave Ivy a strange sense of relief that she wasn't the only passenger who found the ride terrifying, but at the same time it confirmed her belief that her life was indeed in peril.

The air was sticky and hot. Passengers were packed in like cattle. Some sat three to a seat; others stood in the aisle, gripping the handrails and swaying with the movement of the vehicle. The steamy heat only worsened the pungent smells permeating the air—everything from rank body odor to diesel fumes to the rich coffee beans the old woman carried in the sack at her feet. Even the lush vegetation, carved gorges and occasional stunning waterfall failed to distract Ivy from the odors. She was too busy keeping her stomach in check to appreciate the dramatic scenery that surrounded her.

The linen pantsuit she'd donned back in New York had seemed a good choice at the time, but after hours of traveling, it was wrinkled beyond recognition. Perspiration trickled between her breasts, and her shirt stuck uncomfortably to her back. Her feet, clad in a pair of slip-on sandals, ached.

A sudden waft of air through the bus brought with it

the strong smell of spicy jalapenos, and Ivy's stomach roiled alarmingly in response. Stifling a curse, she dug through her handbag until she found what remained of a roll of antacids. She brushed away crumbs from the exposed end, unwrapped the last three tablets and popped them into her mouth, praying the chalky substance would help her queasiness subside. The bus driver had assured her they were going to Pancho Viejo, but she hadn't expected the trip to take so long. She pulled out her itinerary, which was crumpled from handling. After unfolding it, she read through it swiftly.

Arrive Veracruz, Mexico. Okay, she'd managed that part, having departed New York City some fourteen hours earlier aboard an AeroMexico flight, with only a brief layover in Mexico City.

Take public bus to Pancho Viejo. She'd managed that, too. Well, so far. It was anyone's guess when or if she'd make it safely to her destination.

Obtain local transport from Pancho Viejo to Hacienda la Esperanza. Just where *was* Pancho Viejo, anyway? If the bus ride was any indication, the place was somewhere in the dense mountain region north of Veracruz.

The events that had led to this moment had unfolded so quickly she hadn't even had time to do an Internet search about the region before her agent had hustled her off to the airport. She'd been back in New York less than a week, having just wrapped up a film shoot in Montreal, when he had called with the mind-blowing news.

Ivy had been too stunned to question why Finn Mac-Dougall wanted to cast *her* in his latest movie, opposite Hollywood's golden boy, Eric Terrell. If she hadn't actually touched the contract with her own hands, she'd have thought somebody was playing a bad joke on her.

Finn MacDougall wasn't just a great director. In the

hallowed studios of Hollywood, he was king, with a reputation for filmmaking rivaled only by Steven Spielberg's. Barely forty years old, he had it all: a gorgeous wife, two adorable kids and a house overlooking the Pacific worth seven figures.

According to Ivy's agent, MacDougall had seen her in several small, independent films and thought she'd be perfect for his newest project, *Eye of the Hunter.* The proposed salary had left Ivy speechless. As if there had ever been any doubt Ivy would agree to take the part. A two-time Academy Award–winning director, MacDougall specialized in action movies that were pure adrenaline, with edge-of-your-seat suspense that ensured every picture was an unforgettable experience for the audience. Some of the most acclaimed actors in the business owed their careers to Finn MacDougall.

And he wanted *her.*

Ivy wasn't about to question his motives. Without even reading the script, she knew she wouldn't let this opportunity slip by. She just needed to get to the set before he changed his mind, especially since they'd begun shooting three weeks earlier. That information had surprised her. Obviously, she was a last-minute replacement. Directors normally didn't wait until the eleventh hour to pick their leading ladies.

The two days following MacDougall's offer had been a whirlwind of signing contracts and release forms, obtaining medical clearances and insurance, packing and making travel arrangements. Finally, her agent had driven her to the airport, where, at the last minute, he'd thrust a large envelope into her arms.

"It's the script, darling," he'd told her. "You have a nine-hour flight. Do yourself a favor and read it."

She had. Three times, using a lime-green highlighter

to underscore all her lines. The story was about a Special Forces soldier, Garrett Stokes, who'd been taken prisoner by a ruthless drug cartel in Colombia, then rescued by a beautiful missionary. It had more than captured her imagination; it had held her spellbound.

Initially, the script, with its graphic violence and no-holds-barred depiction of covert warfare, had disturbed her. At one point she'd had to put it down and pull several deep breaths in order to control her emotions. The screenplay touched a place within her that was still raw, dragging old memories out from where she'd kept them carefully hidden for two years.

Even now, thoughts of her older brother, Devon, brought an ache to her heart. That he'd died doing something he loved didn't matter. It couldn't dispel the anger and grief she had felt at his loss. She'd arrived at the military hospital in Washington, D.C., shortly after he'd emerged from surgery. Despite the severity of his wounds, she hadn't believed he would die. He'd always been so confident, able to handle anything life threw at him. With the death of their mother four years earlier, he'd been the only family she'd had left. He'd always promised her that he'd come back from Iraq in one piece, that he'd always be there for her. She'd believed it—right up until the moment he'd died.

Devon had wanted to join the marines for as long as Ivy could remember. He'd enlisted on his eighteenth birthday, and nothing had given him as much pride as wearing that uniform. He'd served three tours in Iraq, but his career had come to a tragic and bloody end the day a roadside bomb had shattered his convoy. He'd survived long enough to be airlifted to Landstuhl Hospital in

Germany, then to the Walter Reed Army Medical Center, where he'd finally succumbed to his injuries.

Ivy thought he would have approved of the script she now held in her hands. Her own feelings aside, she acknowledged that the story held a universal appeal. Guys would love it for all the military pyrotechnics, everything from exploding cars to buildings to aircraft. Not to mention some graphically brutal torture scenes. Women would appreciate the romance in the film, especially the love scenes featuring a naked Eric Terrell as the special-ops soldier who falls in love with the missionary who saves his life. Women around the world would faint in their seats at the sight of Eric's cobblestone abs and supremely sculpted arms, not to mention his superior posterior.

Ivy felt a little faint herself at the knowledge that *she* would be on the receiving end of his manly caresses. Thank God she'd maintained her daily exercise regimen in Montreal. Nothing worse than playing opposite the most desired man in America while your thighs jiggled with cellulite.

Not that she was interested in Eric Terrell other than professionally. The last thing she needed was to become involved with yet another leading man. She'd been there, done that, and it had led to only heartache.

There'd been Jacques, the artistic Frenchman she'd thought was totally into her, until she'd discovered he was more into himself. Then there'd been Simon. He'd played a deliciously sexy bad-boy hero, but his naughty habits had extended into his private life to the degree that he'd been unable to commit to just one woman. Finally, there had been Malcolm. She'd completely fallen for his charm, and had believed him when he'd told her she was the only girl for him. It had been the truth, at least while they'd worked on the same project. But once filming had ended, so had his interest in her.

As she looked back on those disastrous affairs, her only excuse was that she'd really believed she was in love. She just hadn't realized that her leading men had been heroes only in the films they were shooting. They'd morphed into complete jerks once they'd returned to the "real" world.

Still, she couldn't help but wonder what it would be like to work so closely with an actor whose reputation made her own appear tame by comparison. Eric Terrell's risqué love affairs were continual fodder for the tabloids, upstaged only by his public displays of temper. He'd once dangled an overly ambitious photographer from a tenth-floor balcony for trying to take his picture. Of course, Eric had also been cheating on his then-fiancée that night, and hadn't been too thrilled about having *those* particular photos made public.

The bus pitched to the right, and Ivy flung out a hand to steady herself, praying the nightmarish ride would soon be over. As if to mock her, the overcast skies opened up, releasing a torrent of rain so heavy that Ivy could no longer see the dense vegetation on either side of the road. Water sprayed in through the open window, soaking her as she struggled with the latch until she finally succeeded in closing the window against the onslaught.

She thought of her tapestry suitcases, strapped to the roof, and all her belongings inside, getting completely soaked. The bus began to slow down, but the hammering rains prevented her from seeing why. Several minutes later, the vehicle shuddered to a stop and the driver stood up, grabbing a little umbrella from beneath his seat.

"Pancho Viejo!" he called, and several people rose

and began pushing their way through the passengers in the aisle.

Ivy rose, as well, clutching her carry-on bag to her chest as she struggled to squeeze around the old woman beside her.

"Con permiso," she murmured, squeezing past the woman and trying not crush the coffee beans underfoot. She worked her way to the front of the bus, but halted in the doorway, reluctant to step out into the deluge. She hugged her bag closer in an attempt to protect the script inside from becoming completely ruined. Then, with a deep breath, she exited the bus.

The force of the tropical downpour took her breath away, blinding her as it slapped against her face and plastered her clothing to her skin. Grimacing at the mud swirling around her feet, she peered toward the roof of the bus, where her suitcases were strapped down. Shielding her eyes, she thought she could just make out the driver crawling along the top.

She was unprepared when a piece of luggage came hurtling off the bus to land squarely in the red soup at her feet and splash her with mud.

"Oh!" She jumped back just in time to avoid a second suitcase pitched over the side. This one, a floral tapestry bag, bounced once then split open, exposing its contents to the torrential downpour. "Hey!" she cried indignantly. "That was my suitcase!"

The bus driver climbed down from the roof, and without glancing in her direction, clambered back aboard the bus. Ivy stepped over to the first suitcase and bent over it, studying the blue vinyl exterior before jerking upright.

This one was *not* her suitcase.

A swift look around showed no other luggage sink-

ing into the mud, which meant her second suitcase
was still secured to the roof. Even as she watched, the
engines throbbed into life and the vehicle began to
slowly pull away.

"Hey, wait!" Ivy started toward the door of the bus,
but was abruptly halted when the thick mud refused to
release her foot. Staring in desperation at the retreating
bus, she gave her foot a yank. With a sucking sound, it
pulled free from the slip-on sandal, which remained
entrapped in the churning muck. Ivy grimaced as she
half ran, half hopped after the bus.

"Wait! My suitcase!" Grasping her overnight bag in
one arm, she frantically waved her free arm, but knew
the likelihood of the bus driver's seeing her was slim to
none.

When the bus finally vanished into the driving rain
and surrounding forest, Ivy stopped, her shoulders
sagging in defeat. *Great.* Her larger suitcase had contained the majority of her clothing and cosmetics. The
smaller suitcase, now lying open to the elements like a
split melon, held mostly her underclothes, nightwear
and three swimsuits.

Peering through the torrent, she saw she'd been de-
posited at the beginning of a narrow road that was little
more than a rutted path through the dense undergrowth.
A low stone wall curving alongside it was the only
other sign of civilization. The bus driver had said this
was Pancho Viejo, but there wasn't so much as a shanty
in sight. How was she supposed to get to the hacienda?
The passengers who had disembarked before her had
seemingly melted into the surrounding vegetation,
leaving Ivy completely alone. A hundred different
thoughts raced through her mind, each one more disturbing than the last. Impossible as it seemed, the bus

had left her in the middle of nowhere. Pushing down her rising panic, Ivy turned back to her suitcase—and stopped dead in her tracks.

Despite the deluge of rain, the man was hard to miss. He was bending over her damaged luggage and it looked as if he was rifling through her belongings.

With a gasp of indignation, Ivy swiped the wet hair back from her eyes and blinked rapidly as the rain pelted her face. If the man was aware of her presence, he gave no indication, and Ivy was torn between confronting him and slinking into the vegetation in hope that he wouldn't notice her. Were there bandits in Mexico? Or, worse, guerrillas? Surely Finn MacDougall wouldn't shoot a movie in a dangerous area. Would he?

She wished now she'd spent more time paying attention to world events and less time reading the celebrity pages of the newspaper. Her imagination surged with all kinds of lurid scenarios. She could almost see the headlines: B-List Actress Abducted By Mexican Bandits. Wealthy Director Refuses To Pay Ransom.

As she stood there, uncertain and wary, the man swiveled his head in her direction. With his eyes still on her, he flipped her small suitcase shut, then lifted it and tucked it beneath his arm, pressing it against his body to keep it closed. He rose slowly to his feet. Dark-red mud clung to the suitcase and stained his white shirt, running in rivulets down his pant legs, like blood.

Despite the fact that he stood perfectly still, the air around him thrummed with energy, like the hum of high-voltage current. Even through the downpour, she felt his eyes on her.

She shivered.

They stared at each other for a long moment, before Ivy gestured helplessly at the piece of luggage he carried.

"That's—that's my suitcase you have there," she said, struggling to keep her voice from wobbling. "There's nothing in it except lingerie. I—I doubt it will fit you." She had a insane urge to giggle at the idea of this man donning her intimate apparel. When his expression didn't change, she instantly sobered. "But you can keep it if you want to."

He didn't answer—he probably didn't even speak English. His black hair was long and framed a jaw covered by at least two days' worth of dark growth. He reached up and pushed his fingers through his hair to slick it back from his square forehead. Rain sluiced down the chiseled planes of his face and glistened on his cheekbones and throat. His soaked white shirt was plastered against his body. Through the thin material, she could see every ridge of muscle that layered his chest and stomach.

The wet fabric emphasized the wide thrust of his shoulders and the impressive bulge of his biceps as he held her suitcase. He wore a pair of khaki cargo pants, also soaked, that hugged his trim hips and strong thighs.

He bent to where her sandal was anchored in the mud and plucked it free. Dangling it from the end of one finger, he began walking toward her.

Ivy shifted her weight. The toes of her bare foot squished in the soggy ground and her wet clothing clung to her skin, but she barely noticed. She hugged her overnight bag tighter against her chest and watched him approach. He had a slightly uneven gait, but she couldn't tell if he was limping or he was compensating for the awkward suitcase he carried.

Despite his dark hair and tanned skin, he didn't really look like a bandit. At least, he didn't look like the Mexican bandits she'd seen in any Hollywood movie, unless you counted *Zorro,* she amended silently.

The guy was a total hunk.

As he drew closer, she realized he was bigger than she'd first thought. It wasn't so much his height—he was probably just over six feet—but he radiated strength. He could probably bench-press her with one hand and never break a sweat.

She swallowed hard.

He stopped less than a foot away, and it was only then that she noted there wasn't anything remotely Mexican about him. Unless, of course, you counted his eyes, which were such a light shade of brown that they reminded Ivy of Aztec gold. As she stared at him, something stirred deep in her subconscious—a recognition of sorts. She couldn't put her finger on it, but his eyes disturbed her. And right now, they were traveling over her in a way that could only be called predatory.

Hungry.

Ivy shivered and her heart rate kicked into overdrive. Her breathing quickened and she was acutely conscious of a fight-or-flight response surfacing within her. But even more alarming was her awareness of the male appreciation in this man's heated eyes, and that secretly she thrilled to it.

As his gaze traveled lazily over her, a small voice urged her to neither fight nor flee, but surrender willingly to whatever it was he might have in mind for her.

2

GARRETT STOKES KNEW he made her nervous, but, damn, he couldn't stop staring at her. He knew he should introduce himself, assure her that Finn Mac-Dougall had sent him to transport her to the Hacienda la Esperanza. But the ability to form words had suddenly abandoned him. Seeing Ivy James in the flesh exceeded every erotic fantasy he'd ever had about her, and he'd had his share.

She stood watching him with a mixture of apprehension and curiosity in her wide eyes. The rain plastered her dark hair to her head in a sleek cap, while her clothing had taken on the appearance of wet tissue paper. Too bad she'd shifted her overnight bag around to her front. He'd really appreciated the view before she'd hidden her body from his sight.

She was taller than he remembered, and more slender, but her eyes were what really did it to him. Looking into them was like having somebody sucker punch him in the gut.

He felt winded and a little weak.

He couldn't recall having had this reaction to her the first time he'd seen her two years earlier. Then again, he'd been too busted up and hazy from the pain meds they'd given him to feel much of anything. But his own injuries had been insignificant compared with those of the soldier in the bed next to his at the Walter Reed Army Medical Center. Devon James had been a tank gunner deployed with the 10th Marine Regiment in Iraq when an IED—an improvised explosive device—had hit his convoy. The explosion had taken his right arm and shredded his body. He'd lain in bed with wires and tubes protruding from what remained of him.

On Devon's second day at Walter Reed, his sister had arrived at the hospital, pale but determined, reassuring her brother that he'd be okay. Devon had been conscious, but heavily sedated. Through the gap in the curtain that had separated their beds, Garrett had observed her. Even in his own foggy state, he'd thought her beautiful. Her calm demeanor had been so impressive; he'd almost believed she could be right and that her brother *would* survive. But when she'd left the room to confer with one of the doctors, her brother had turned his face toward Garrett.

"I'm not going to make it, man," he'd said, his voice little more than a whisper. "She won't accept it, though. Always was a stubborn brat."

"Hang in there," Garrett had croaked.

"No, man," Devon had said, closing his eyes. "It's no good. I worry what's going to happen to her when I'm gone. She'll be alone."

"There must be someone," he'd responded. "Some family or friend."

"No. It was just the two of us."

Garrett had been silent. He couldn't make a promise to watch over some chick he didn't even know, no matter how gorgeous she was. Besides, she appeared more than capable of taking care of herself.

"I'll keep an eye on her."

Devon had looked over at him, and Garrett had

flinched at the hope he'd seen flare in his gaze. "You swear? She doesn't even have to know. Just do it for me."

"I swear."

Less than three hours later, while his sister had looked on in dismay, Sergeant Devon James had flat-lined. Nurses had hustled Ivy out of the room while medical personnel had tried to resuscitate her brother, but their efforts had been futile.

The weight of Garrett's promise had settled heavily onto his shoulders, but it had also given him something to live for. He'd latched on to the promise with all the desperation of a drowning man clinging to a lifeline, determined to be there for the girl in the future.

Now here he was, two years later, standing in front of the woman he'd promised to keep an eye on, completely kicking himself that he'd never made contact with her before now. Back then, just the knowledge that she might someday need him had been enough of an incentive to push him to recover. Throughout the long months of rehabilitation, he'd followed her career. He'd kept tabs on her activities and had been prepared to step in and help her if necessary, but an opportunity had never arisen.

Until now.

He should say something to her, tell her about his connection to her, if you could even call it that. Instead, he stared speechlessly, wondering how she would react if she knew the truth. Ivy James had saved his soul, and she wasn't even aware of it.

He still wasn't sure how he felt about having his combat experiences made into an action-adventure movie, but there was one thing he'd always been certain of: he'd wanted Ivy James to play the part of the leading lady. It was just one way he could fulfill the promise he'd made to her brother.

When Garrett's brother-in-law, Finn MacDougall, had initially approached him about the venture, he'd adamantly refused to give his consent. He still had nightmares about those last horrific days in Colombia when a covert narcoterrorism mission had come apart like a five-dollar shirt.

He'd allowed himself to be captured in order to provide the rest of his team a chance to escape. It had worked, but the three days he'd endured in the hands of the brutal Escudero cartel had just about sapped his belief in the goodness of mankind. It wasn't so much what they'd done to his body that had nearly killed him; it was what they'd done to his spirit.

If anybody knew just how tough his recovery had been, it was Finn. After all, Garrett had spent nearly a year living in Finn's home while recuperating from injuries that included multiple gunshot and stab wounds. His body still bore the scars from where he'd been tortured by the cartel. Despite having pushed himself to the max to regain his strength, he had to live with the knowledge that his abilities were now compromised to the point where he'd never again serve as part of a Green Beret "A-Team," the twelve-man basic unit that could carry out any number of deadly covert operations.

Even after he'd managed to escape, two more days had passed before he'd found refuge, then another six days before he'd been airlifted out of the steaming Colombian jungle to an American hospital. His only satisfaction was knowing the information he'd brought back with him had been enough for the Colombian military to target the cartel and put an end to their reign of terror and drug smuggling.

Now, looking at the woman who would play Helena Vanderveer, the Dutch missionary responsible for rescuing his sorry ass, he wondered if he'd been wrong. There was a sensuality about Ivy James that was undeniable, yet at the same time she looked so god-damned…fragile. The real Helena might fool some with her small stature and sweet smile, but beneath it all she was as tough as Kevlar. Nobody could ever call her fragile.

Ivy was still staring at him. As he tried to formulate the right words to introduce himself, the rain suddenly stopped, and a warm burst of sunlight fell over the spot where they stood. Ivy tilted her face up toward the clearing skies and smiled.

Garrett felt something in his chest shift.

"Oh, wow," she breathed. "It's over. Just like that."

She turned her gaze back to Garrett. Her eyes were the same rich, dark-chocolate shade he remembered, thickly fringed with spiky dark lashes. She used her fingers to wipe the moisture from her face as she again focused on the suitcase he carried.

"La maleta…la sandalia," she said haltingly. A small frown creased her forehead as she pointed first toward the luggage, then toward the sandal he held. *"Es mina."*

Her pronunciation was terrible, her grammar worse. But even if he hadn't spoken Spanish fluently, there was no mistaking her meaning. Glancing down at the mud-covered shoe that still dangled from his hand, he swiped it against the wet fabric of his cargo pants until most of the mud was gone, then handed it to her.

"Yeah, I know they're yours."

"Oh! You speak English! That's great." Her face cleared as she accepted the shoe, and then she balanced on one leg as she slid her bare, mud-covered foot into the sandal. "For a second, I wasn't sure if you understood me."

Garrett smiled. "I'm American. Finn sent me to meet you." He gestured over his shoulder at the rutted lane that intersected the main road. "I have a Jeep parked just down there. I'll drive you out to the hacienda."

"Thank God!" she exclaimed, and Garrett saw all the tension leave her body. "I really thought I was going to be stranded out here in the middle of nowhere, and then I saw you and—"

He watched with interest as her cheeks pinkened.

"Well, let's just say I envisioned the worst," she admitted, tucking a wet strand of hair behind one ear and slinging her carry-on bag over her shoulder. "You must be part of the film crew." She tilted her head and considered him for a moment. "Do I know you? Have we met before? You seem familiar to me."

Garrett hesitated, momentarily at a loss for words. Shifting her bag to her other shoulder had brought her luscious breasts fully into view. Beneath the wet fabric of her sleeveless top, he could clearly see her bra and, beneath that, the dark shadow of her nipples. His throat went dry, and he had to drag his gaze from her and turn away.

"Ah, no," he finally managed to say, keeping his voice neutral. "I'm a technical consultant. Let me grab your other bag, and then we can head out."

"Oh, that's not my suitcase." She laid a hand on his arm to stop him. "The driver threw down the wrong one and took off before I could tell him."

Garrett glanced at her hand. She jerked it back, but he could still feel her slender fingers against his skin. Briefly, he wondered how they would feel against other parts of his anatomy.

"We'll take it along with us," he said over his shoulder. "It's unlikely yours will be returned, but just in case, we'll have someone bring this back to the airport in Veracruz and put in a claim for your bag."

With any luck, her second travel case wouldn't show up. Ever. He'd spent only a second or two shoving her spilled belongings back into the ruined suitcase, but that had been long enough for him to realize the case contained mostly underwear and shit, girly stuff not meant to be worn in public. His hands had skimmed over wet satin panties and lacy bras, silky pajamas and fragile camisole tops, all soaked from the rain. His imagination soared with tantalizing images of a barely clad Ivy. He had no problem whatsoever with her wearing nothing but underwear for the entire time she was in Mexico.

Hefting the blue suitcase in one arm and still holding her tapestry bag under his other, he made his way to where he'd parked the Jeep, acutely aware of the woman following closely behind him.

Watching him.

For the first time since he'd been released from the hospital, after months of excruciating physical therapy to finally get rid of his damn crutches, he felt self-conscious about his limp. He knew he was lucky even to have use of his leg, but he hadn't quite resigned himself to the limp now being as much a part of the "new" him as the scars that went with it.

"How long will it take to get to the hacienda?" Ivy asked, as he stowed her gear behind the passenger seat and held the door open for her to climb in.

"Not long. About ten minutes." He rounded the hood of the Jeep and slid into the driver's seat, using his hand to help lift his bad leg into the vehicle. He didn't meet her eyes as he started the engine. There were a lot of expressions he'd like to see in those big, dark eyes, but sympathy wasn't one of them.

"I like the name. Hacienda la Esperanza," she said experimentally. "It sounds…beautiful."

"The place started out in the sixteenth century as a monastery," he said, maneuvering the Jeep along the rough road. "Then it was used as a coffee plantation, before being abandoned about thirty years ago. Now it's privately owned, and mostly used for retreats or special events. Weddings. Reunions. That kind of thing."

"Oh."

Garrett couldn't tell what her expectations were, but suspected she'd be pleasantly surprised by the hacienda. With over one hundred rooms on two levels, it was a masterpiece of classic Spanish architecture. Rooms that had once housed Jesuit seminarians had been converted into elegant spaces with most of the original architectural features, including arched windows and heavily beamed ceilings. The only indulgence had been the addition of private marble baths in each room.

The hacienda had been chosen not only because it could accommodate the entire cast and crew, but because the property itself, as well as the mountainous region surrounding it, closely resembled Colombia.

Garrett had spent his first two nights in the monastery-turned-hacienda, but the vast hallways and vaulted ceilings made him feel exposed. He preferred the old workers' quarters behind the house, a series of *casitas,* or cottages. Each *casita* consisted of a simple wooden platform with wood walls and a tin roof. He'd cleared a host of small scorpions and spiders out of one of the cottages, and the production crew had acquired some basic furniture and a couple of kerosene lanterns for him. It was sparse, but comfortable. In it, Garrett could enjoy the solitude of the nearby forest and avoid the endless noise and activity of the main house.

The set director and his crew had divided the property into several separate filming locations. One area served as the Dutch mission where Helena Vanderveer worked, complete with small chapel. The design folks had done almost too good a job at transforming the derelict warehouse located on the premises into a replica of the cartel stronghold where he'd been held and tortured.

Garrett glanced over at Ivy.

She was sitting upright, trying not to let her back touch the seat, and he knew her wet clothing must be uncomfortable. Despite the humid warmth of the afternoon, he could see goose bumps on her bare arms.

"You need to get out of those wet clothes," he commented. "One of the girls in the makeup department is about your size. Maybe you can borrow something from her until we get your own wardrobe figured out."

She cast him a grateful glance. "That would be great." She was silent for a moment. "So what's it like on the set? I mean, everyone else has been on location for three weeks. I can't help but feel like—like an intruder."

He knew she was referring to the fact that she'd been offered the role only two days earlier. Although Finn had given his word that he would cast Ivy as Helena Vanderveer, he'd held off actually making the offer until the very last minute, no doubt hoping Garrett would change his mind and let him offer the part to some A-list actress who, when paired with Eric Terrell, would guarantee record-breaking crowds at the theaters.

No freaking way.

Garrett had wanted Ivy James. Okay, so he'd had an ulterior motive, but his own lust for her aside, he'd seen every film she'd ever made and knew she'd do justice to Finn's project. Her previous work had consisted of almost exclusively small, independent films, but her performances had been impressive. The only reservations Finn had had about bringing her onto this project had nothing to do with her acting.

Of course, Ivy James did have a history of falling in love with her leading men. With the exception of her two most recent films, she had become romantically involved with several of her male costars, although the relationships had never seemed to last beyond filming.

But it wasn't her failed love affairs that had made Finn hesitate. It was the fact that despite her talents, she was a relative unknown. Her prior flicks hadn't garnered wide distribution. She was a risk, and if not for Garrett's insistence, Finn probably wouldn't have considered her for the part.

Garrett glanced over at Ivy again, unwilling to tell her why Finn had waited until the last minute to contact her agent. She'd accepted the part. She didn't need to know the circumstances surrounding the offer.

"Finn probably would have approached your agent sooner, but he didn't want to distract you from the project you were wrapping up in Montreal," he lied. "I know that he's eager to meet you. They'll begin shooting your scenes in just a couple of days."

"Have you—have you worked with Eric Terrell before?"

Her tone was casual, but Garrett didn't miss the underlying anxiety. He noted the color in her cheeks and the way she clenched the strap of her carry-on bag. She was nervous about meeting the acclaimed actor, and he couldn't really blame her. The guy was on the front page of every tabloid and at the top of every media list there was. *Hottest Actor. Most Eligible Bachelor. Sexiest Man Alive.*

They'd forgotten to add *Biggest Dickhead On The Planet,* but Garrett guessed that most folks who knew him already had that one figured out. He'd shown up on location with an entourage of support personnel, including a bodyguard, a personal secretary and his own makeup person. Hell, the production company had even agreed to pay for a private cook for him. He'd put up a huge stink when he'd learned he'd be working with a relatively unknown actress. He'd actually told Finn he would only star opposite an A-list actress. Garrett had to give his brother-in-law credit. Finn hadn't backed down. Instead, he'd calmly told Eric that he could get over it or get off his set. Eric had buttoned his mouth, but Garrett knew the decision had rankled. He hoped to hell the other man would maintain his pompous-ass mind-set and leave Ivy the hell alone, but he doubted he'd get that lucky. With her looks, Ivy would be pure temptation.

Garrett never would have chosen Terrell to portray him in the film, but Finn had insisted the choice was a good one. During the past three weeks, Garrett had reluctantly acknowledged he was right. Based on the uncut footage he'd seen so far, he'd say Finn had another blockbuster in the making.

"This is the first time I've worked with him." He was carefully noncommittal.

Ivy flashed him a smile. "I've seen his movies." She gave a self-conscious laugh. "I mean, who *hasn't* seen his movies, right? I just never thought I'd get the chance to work with him. I'd have thought they'd want somebody like Angelina Jolie or Jessica Alba for this part."

Garrett let his gaze slide over her. "Trust me," he drawled, "there was never any question about you being cast for this part."

Her eyes widened fractionally and then filled with pleasure before she looked out the window, hiding her expression from him. But Garrett could still see the smile that hovered on her lips, and he felt a ridiculous sense of satisfaction knowing he'd put it there. His eyes lingered on her a moment, noting how her hair was beginning to dry in soft corkscrews around her face. He wondered how the curls would feel in his hands. His fingers tightened on the steering wheel, and he forced himself to focus on his driving.

"I've worked so hard at my career," she continued. "True, a lot of people would say my choice of films has been a little unorthodox, but I've always tried to choose roles that would challenge me, you know?"

He glanced over at her. "Sure."

"I mean, I've been offered plenty of roles in popcorn movies, but I want to be taken seriously." She turned earnest eyes to him. "That's why this role is so exciting. It means I'm finally reaching that point in my career where people are starting to sit up and notice." She smiled. "I just never thought my past projects would capture the attention of a director like Finn MacDougall. It's more than I could've ever hoped for."

Garrett determinedly ignored the guilt that rose in him and gave her a polite smile of acknowledgment. "I'm certain you won't let him down."

She laughed. "Not if I can help it. I'll do whatever is necessary to make this the best performance of my career."

The dense foliage fell away as they entered the tiny

village of Pancho Viejo, a cluster of small houses and rustic buildings that circled a central plaza with an ornate fountain. Carefully manicured trees lined the narrow road, their trunks painted white and their branches strung with colorful lights. The picturesque scene elicited a murmur of delight from Ivy.

They turned off the small road and drove through a set of old, iron gates, then along a road less rutted than the one they had just traveled. Slowly, the thick vegetation on either side of the road gave way to steep, tiered hillsides still bearing traces of the coffee bean cultivation that had supported generations of local residents. Before long, the hills leveled out. Garrett suppressed a smile as Ivy caught her first glimpse of Hacienda la Esperanza and gasped.

Situated at the end of a long drive bordered on either side by fig and cypress trees, the hacienda was a sprawling, two-story structure of white stucco. Tall, narrow windows marched along the first and second floors. Creeping ivy clung to the near side of the building, completely obscuring the white stucco, insinuating itself into the window embrasures and dangling in long ropes from the overhanging roof. The sun was sinking behind a panoramic backdrop of lush mountains, streaking the skies with warm hues of orange and pink, and Garrett admitted the house made a stunning first impression.

Skirting the building, he drove around to the back of the hacienda. The circular drive stopped in front of a covered walkway supported by stone pillars and flanked on either side by lush gardens.

As he pulled onto the gravel lot, the sound of laughter and muted conversation drifted toward them. Garrett eyed his watch. It was almost nine o'clock. Congregating by the pool after dinner to discuss the day's filming over drinks, before going to bed, had become something of a ritual for the cast.

Ivy stood close by his side as he hauled her suitcase out of the Jeep, and he caught her looking speculatively toward the house. Her clothing still clung damply to her skin, and the thought of parading her past the other cast members held little appeal for him. No way did he want Eric Terrell to see Ivy in her current state. That Ivy would be shooting some pretty intimate love scenes with the actor didn't matter. To Garrett's way of thinking, her nearly transparent clothing was almost more erotic than if she was butt naked.

Okay, that was a complete lie.

Just the thought of Ivy James in the nude made his body tighten in response.

"C'mon," he said, his voice more brusque than he'd intended. "I'll show you to your room and then ask Denise, who works in makeup, to find you something dry to wear."

She cast him a grateful glance and walked ahead of him down the covered walkway and into the large, central courtyard. A fountain gurgled in the center, surrounded by lush gardens. The hacienda rose up on all sides. What had once been the cloisters had been converted into private balconies overlooking the gardens.

"Up these stairs to the left," he murmured, indicating the winding stone staircase that connected the two floors of the hacienda and led to the private rooms on the second level.

Garrett followed at a slower pace, not even trying to force his bad leg to move faster. He knew from bitter experience that would do no good, and he'd just be sore and sorry the following day. Besides, being several steps behind Ivy gave him the opportunity to admire her perfect, heart-shaped rear as she climbed the steps.

They reached the upper level of the hacienda, and he preceded her along an interior corridor with vaulted ceilings and tiled floors. He stopped in front of an ornately carved door at the end of the hallway.

"This is your room." He pushed open the door and set her luggage just inside. "It has a nice view of the mountains. I'll go find Denise and get you those dry clothes. When you've changed, just come back down the stairs and follow the voices to the pool area, okay?"

"Wait." She faced him. "I'm sorry," she blurted, "but I don't even know your name. You've gone out of your way to be so nice to me, and I can't believe I haven't even asked your name."

"It's Garrett Stokes."

"Garrett—"

She broke off, and Garrett knew the exact instant she realized who he was.

"Oh, my God," she breathed. "You're *him*. The special-ops guy this movie is all about."

Garrett allowed himself a wry smile. "Yes, ma'am."

She'd had absolutely no clue who he was. He wasn't surprised that she had no recollection of him. She'd definitely had bigger things on her mind than some injured soldier who'd shared hospital space with her brother. Nevertheless, he still found it disconcerting that in those few hours, she'd made a profound impact on his life, while he hadn't even registered on her radar. He wouldn't betray her brother's trust by telling her that he'd been that soldier, since doing so would be equivalent to opening Pandora's box. But a part of him still wanted to create a ripple in her world, make her as aware of him as he was of her.

She frowned. "I thought you were a technical consultant."

He shrugged. "I am. Finn brought me aboard to ensure the film captures my covert-ops experiences as realistically as possible."

Her face paled, and Garrett could tell she was remembering the gruesome torture scenes. He'd seen the storyboards and read the script. The screenwriter hadn't spared the audience when he'd written those portions of the screenplay.

As quickly as the color had drained from her cheeks, it flooded back. "The scenes with the missionary—are they based on real life, as well?"

Garrett hesitated.

She was referring to the explicit, highly sensual love scenes. He fought briefly with his conscience, debating whether to tell her the truth. They were the one facet of the movie that didn't conform to events as he'd experienced them. Finn had insisted on taking artistic license in portraying Helena Vanderveer as a beautiful young woman with a healthy libido and an instant attraction to the injured soldier who'd found his way to her mission.

In reality, Helena was a sturdy Dutch woman in her midsixties, with a strong spiritual calling and zero interest in any romantic entanglements. Furthermore, Garrett had been unconscious most of the time she'd cared for him. He had only hazy memories of her and their time together.

Finn had brushed all that aside, insisting a torrid love affair between the soldier and the missionary would heighten the film's appeal. At his request, the writer had revised the script to depict the soldier as badly injured, but not to the extent that he couldn't engage in some creative lovemaking with the attractive missionary. *Never underestimate the healing powers of lust,* Garrett thought wryly.

"Pretty much everything in the script is accurate," he fibbed, boldly meeting Ivy's eyes, "especially the scenes with Helena."

"Oh." She was silent as she digested his words, and the color in her cheeks deepened. "Well, I hope I can do your…relationship…justice."

Garrett kept his face carefully impassive. "Don't worry. I'll let you know if you're not getting it right."

Her eyes grew big. "You're not—you're not actually going to be on the set while we shoot *those* scenes…are you?"

Garrett heard the horror in her voice, and only barely suppressed a grin. "You bet."

"Why?" She sounded desperate.

"Just in case you need any pointers," he responded guilelessly. "It's my job to make certain every scene is shot as realistically as possible."

"Why would I need *pointers* from you?"

"Because every woman responds differently to a man's touch," Garrett replied, allowing his gaze to drift over Ivy's body. "And despite the fact that you're shooting the scenes with Eric Terrell, you'll have to respond as if you're with *me.*"

He left her standing wide-eyed and mute in the doorway of her bedroom. But as he turned away, he saw with satisfaction the beginnings of something else in her dark eyes, and he smiled.

That something was awareness.

3

TWENTY MINUTES LATER, Ivy stood by the pool with a margarita in one hand as Finn MacDougall shook her other hand and apologized for his rudeness in waiting until the last possible minute to offer her the role. He had indeed not wanted to distract her from the project she'd been involved in. He'd meant to contact her sooner, but time had gotten away from him. He was thrilled to have her on location, and excited to begin working with her.

Dazed, Ivy could only listen and nod and smile like an idiot. Finn was every bit as charismatic and artistic as she'd imagined he would be, and she was tempted to pinch herself to ensure the whole thing wasn't a dream. How was it possible that Finn MacDougall was apologizing to *her?*

The entire scene was like something in a bad comedy, and completely opposite to how she'd envisioned her first meeting with the famed director. In her endless imaginings, she'd been composed, casually elegant and regally gracious. She certainly hadn't looked like something the cat had dragged in.

Her hair was almost dry, but the humidity caused it to curl into an unruly tangle. She hadn't had time to freshen her makeup, and she knew she looked tired and pale. Worse, the clothing that Denise had loaned her made her feel like a grungy teenager. Denise herself had been little more than a petulant adolescent, clearly put out by Ivy's needing to borrow her clothes.

"Here," she'd snapped. "It's all I can spare. You'll have to talk to the wardrobe people for any other clothes."

She'd flounced out of Ivy's room without another word. Ivy had reluctantly changed into the clothing, and cringed when she saw how terrible she appeared in the borrowed outfit, which consisted of a shapeless T-shirt and a pair of baggy pants that suspiciously resembled pajama bottoms.

God, what must Finn think of her?

"Well, it's great to finally meet you," he was saying. "I wish I could stay, but I have an appointment with the assistant director to review the dailies, so just—" he swept a hand toward the people who milled around the pool "—make yourself comfortable. We'll talk again in the morning."

Ivy watched as he made his way back to the main house, stopping several times to speak to people. She'd been hastily introduced to the other cast members, but aside from one or two familiar faces, they were mostly unknown to her. Viewing them now as they chatted and laughed, she was reluctant to insert herself into their intimate conversations.

She swirled her drink uncertainly for a moment, feeling awkward and self-conscious, until her gaze fell on the man at the far side of the terraced patio. Even while talking with Finn, she'd been acutely aware of Garrett Stokes several paces away, observing her.

She couldn't get his last words out of her head: *"You'll have to respond as if you're with me."*

Worse, every time she envisioned herself acting out the love scenes for the movie, Garrett was the man she cast in the leading role. A supremely muscled, naked Garrett, with molten eyes.

Which was crazy. An hour ago, she'd been a jumble of nerves just thinking about working with Eric Terrell. She considered him so far out of her league, both personally and professionally, that she'd had trouble visualizing herself as his on-screen love interest. Now she couldn't even recall what he looked like. The man who came to mind was Garrett Stokes. Maybe it was the knowledge that he was the real deal—the Green Beret who'd experienced everything in the script firsthand. *He* was the one Helena Vanderveer had risked everything for, including her life…and her heart.

Unwillingly, her gaze slid over him. He'd changed out of his wet clothes and now wore a loose-fitting shirt made of some gauzy, breathable material over a dry pair of cargo pants. But even the casual clothing couldn't disguise his wide shoulders or flat stomach, or hide that his was a leanly muscled physique. He exuded a raw sexuality that turned a woman's thoughts to hot, potent kisses and bone-melting orgasms. Despite knowing him less than an hour, Ivy realized she wasn't at all immune to those insidious thoughts.

She wondered what it would be like to be pressed against all that hard warmth. He'd said every woman responded differently to a man's touch—as if he was an expert on the subject. How would she respond to his touch, to his hands on her body and his mouth on her skin?

As though sensing her wayward thoughts, Garrett smiled at her, a slow, knowing smile that caused her breasts to tighten and heat to swamp her midsection. If that was how he'd looked at Helena Vanderveer, no wonder the missionary had torn off her clothes and jumped into the guy's sickbed with him. Ivy felt hot color sweep up her neck to her face, but she was helpless to drag her eyes away from him.

"Hey, you must be Ivy."

Startled, Ivy turned to see an attractive woman in a turquoise sarong smiling at her. Her red hair was an artful disarray of curls, captured in an oversize clip at the back of her head, and her green eyes were elongated by an expert sweep of black eyeliner. She had such an open, friendly face that Ivy couldn't help but smile back at her. The other woman extended her hand.

"I'm Carla Ricci, and I'll be doing your makeup." She gave Ivy an appraising look. "You have great bone structure, and your eyes are *amazing,* but we'll have to do something with the hair. A little conditioner, and you'll be all set."

Ivy grimaced and self-consciously put a hand to her head. "We got caught in a downpour, and I haven't had time to do anything with it," she explained.

"Oh, yes, I heard. You and Mr. Military Badass over there." She rolled her eyes meaningfully in Garrett's direction. "He wanted to drive into Veracruz to pick you up at the airport, but Finn needed him here, instead. I expected the guy to go completely Rambo when he found out you were taking the public bus in." She shuddered. "You poor thing."

"It wasn't that bad," Ivy lied, "except that I lost my luggage."

Carla put a conciliatory hand on Ivy's arm. "I heard." She cast a sympathetic glance at Ivy's outfit. "If your suitcase doesn't show up and you need something to wear, come see me. I have some little dresses that would look totally hot on you, and it would teach Denise a lesson, the little bitch. She's just worried that Eric will find you more attractive than he finds her."

Surprised, Ivy couldn't help but give a small bark of laughter. "Me? Oh, *please*. I've seen the women Eric Terrell is attracted to, and I'm pretty sure I'm not up to those standards."

"Are you kidding?" Carla shot her a look of astonishment. "When's the last time you stood in front of the mirror, sweetie? You totally have a young Julia Ormond look going on, all sweet and sexy at the same time. And those curls are to die for." She caught an errant ringlet on the end of her finger. "Most women would kill for hair like this." She winked at Ivy conspiratorially. "Besides, from what I hear, your leading men have a hard time keeping an arm's length, if you know what I mean. If you ask me, you could have this one eating out of your hands...or more."

Embarrassed by the other woman's candidness, Ivy couldn't help darting a glance at Garrett Stokes, wondering how much of the bizarre conversation he could overhear. She hoped none of it. "Well, I'm definitely just here to do a job, so I doubt there'll be any of *that* going on."

Carla smiled at her knowingly. "I guess we'll just have to wait and find out, won't we? Of course, none of us would be heartbroken if Eric developed a little thing for you, since it would put Denise's nose hugely out of joint, if you get my meaning."

Ivy blinked.

A burst of laughter erupted from those nearest the house, and the cast members sitting by the pool glanced up, suddenly alert.

"Oh, here he is now," Carla said sotto voce. "Good luck, sweetie. See you on the set!"

Ivy turned around expectantly, to find that Eric Terrell had arrived. For him to make his way toward the terrace where she stood took several long moments, giving Ivy the opportunity to study him.

He was without doubt the most beautiful man she'd ever seen. His golden skin glowed with good health, and his teeth flashed white as he laughed at something a woman said to him. His famous hair, long acclaimed by the style press as a masterpiece of tousled honey and wheaten streaks, had been cropped to military standards, but even the quarter inch that remained managed to look like gilded velvet, begging to be stroked. He was every inch the golden boy, and he knew it.

Ivy watched as he ingratiated himself with the other cast members, but she couldn't help feeling his joviality had a falseness. As he drew closer, she heard the deep warmth of his voice, and caught the tail end of an outrageous remark that made those nearest him guffaw anew.

Eric smiled as he moved away from the group, but when he finally stopped in front of Ivy, she could tell the smile didn't reach his eyes. He let his gaze drift over her for a moment, taking in every detail of her disheveled appearance. His beautiful mouth twisted briefly.

"You must be Ivy James."

"Yes." Was it really *her* voice that sounded so breathless? She watched in utter fascination as the pink tip of his tongue probed the corner of his mouth. He assessed her silently for a moment, nodding to himself.

"Okay, okay. I think we can make this work," he finally murmured. "But you might want to wear something…I don't know…more feminine?" He shifted his weight, and Ivy could have sworn his chest had expanded by at least two inches. "You've never worked with me, but those who *have* know that when I'm filming a project, I get completely into character, both on and off camera. I mean *completely*. And if I'm not feeling the love off camera, then it'll show when I'm trying to execute those intimate scenes on camera." He tilted his head. "Are you understanding what I'm saying?"

Ivy shook her head, completely bemused. "No." Out of her peripheral vision, she noticed that Garrett Stokes had moved closer.

Eric scratched the bridge of his nose, clearly struggling with his patience. "Look," he said, as if addressing a three-year-old, "the audience has to believe that the chemistry between us on-screen is the real deal. But in order for me to convey that passion, I need to feel it. I mean *really* feel it." His eyes were a light blue, almost silver. Now they boldly skimmed her body. "I need to be able to relate to you sexually in order to play the love scenes properly. And, babe, that outfit just doesn't do it for me. *Now* do you understand?"

Ivy felt her mouth start to fall open. She snapped it shut. Shock swept through her, rendering her momentarily speechless. When she did find her voice, it came out sounding strangled.

"Unless I'm working, I'll wear whatever I want to wear, *babe,* and I'll wear it for my pleasure, not yours." She was only slightly gratified to note a flush seep over his perfect cheekbones. She pressed on, her voice growing stronger with her increasing irritation. "But I do have one question for you. What if the script called for you to murder me? Would you then need to relate to me on some violent level in order to play the part properly?"

Eric Terrell stared at her for a full minute, during which Ivy was uncomfortably aware of the complete silence that surrounded them. Then he laughed softly.

"Okay," he relented, "so that's how it's going to be." His eyes continued to hold hers, and something in them made her shiver. "I guess I was wrong about you."

"What do you mean?"

He smiled, and his gaze dropped leisurely over her body. "I just figured you'd want to portray your character as realistically as possible." He leaned toward her and said conspiratorially, "Even maintain certain relationships off camera in order for them to strike a realistic chord on camera. Now I *know* you know what I'm talking about."

There was no mistaking the sensual intent in his eyes. Ivy's heart began to pound and she was certain he would hear it thumping in her chest. Instead of feeling flattered by his obvious interest, she felt vaguely panicky and a little cheapened, as if he thought she was an easy lay because of her prior relationships. She'd always known some people would judge her based on her past, but she hadn't thought anyone would be so blatant about it, so insulting. She tried to tell herself that it didn't matter; Eric Terrell was a guy who made a practice of sleeping with his costars, so he probably judged everyone else by his own low standards. As she struggled to formulate a response, a smooth voice cut in from behind her.

"Hey, pal, lighten up. The rest of us have worked with you long enough to know you're just kidding, but I think you're making our leading lady a little uncomfortable." Garrett's voice was easy, but his eyes were hard.

Ivy stopped breathing as the two men stared at each other for a long minute. Garrett's stance was relaxed, and to anyone who watched, the three of them might appear to be having a friendly conversation, but Ivy sensed the tension that coiled inside him.

Finally, Eric snickered. "Yeah, right." He swung his gaze back to Ivy. "No offense. I was just kidding." He leaned toward her, and for a moment Ivy thought he was going to say something in her ear. Instead, he sniffed delicately several times.

Ivy recoiled. He was *smelling* her!

"Just do me a favor and don't wear any scented cosmetics or perfumes, okay?" He stepped back and smiled humorlessly at her, making no effort to keep his voice down. "The smell of that shit makes my stomach turn. Don't make it *too* difficult for me to act like I actually want to do you."

Without another word, he walked away. Almost immediately, the stifled conversation resumed around them. Ivy fought for composure, determined not let the others see her mortification. That he'd actually implied she wasn't attractive enough to turn him on, either on-screen or off, was humiliating enough, but to have done it in front of the other cast members was just unbelievable. She didn't dare look at Garrett. Suppressing a groan, she drained her margarita glass in one lengthy swallow, shuddering at the strong alcohol.

"He's right about one thing." Garrett's voice was pitched low, for her ears alone.

Ivy lowered her glass and reluctantly faced him. His light-brown eyes were the same shade as the aged tequila warming her belly and causing a pleasant glow to spread outward from her center. For just a second she had a crazy belief that if she could just sink into the endless depths of those eyes, she would find the peace and inner strength she so desperately needed right then.

She forced herself to smile at him. No way would she let him know just how seriously Golden Boy had pissed her off. For all she knew, Garrett had handpicked Eric

Terrell for the part. She understood enough about the inner workings of Hollywood to realize that if Garrett complained about her to Finn MacDougall, just one call to the producer and she would be on the next plane back to New York.

"Oh, yeah?" she asked. "What's he right about?"

Whatever she'd been expecting, it wasn't for him to lean in toward her until his face was scant millimeters from her jaw. He breathed deeply, inhaling her scent. When he pulled back, a smile curved his mouth. "You don't need any perfumes. You smell…great…just the way you are."

Ivy stared at him, unable to form a coherent response. He was close enough that she could see the amazing striation of golds and browns in his irises, see the stubble of whiskers that shadowed his lean jaw and the small scar that bisected his upper lip and made her ache to trace her fingertip across it.

His mouth fascinated her. It was a hedonistic mouth, capable of doing wicked things. She could imagine his lips against hers, working magic before working their way down the length of her body. Heat unfurled low in her belly. She stared at his mouth, mesmerized. His gaze fastened on her lips, and as if time itself had slowed, he bent his head fractionally toward hers.

Ivy felt her breath escape on a sigh. She was barely aware of the other cast members congregated around the pool. Her limbs loosened, and warmth slid along her veins. He was going to kiss her, right there in front of everybody, and she didn't even care. Her eyes drifted shut.

"It's been a long day," he said abruptly, his voice rough. "Look at you, falling asleep on your feet."

Ivy's eyes flew open to find he'd pulled back slightly. His expression as he regarded her was unreadable. Hot shame flooded her face. She glanced around swiftly, but if anyone else had guessed how close she'd just come to attaching herself to Garrett Stokes's face, they gave no indication.

She exhaled on a shaky breath and forced herself to smile. "You're right." She pushed a hand through her hair, unable to meet his eyes. She was pathetic. What must he think of her? She needed to get out of there immediately, before she did something really laughable. As if a public confrontation with Eric Terrell hadn't been stupid enough, she'd nearly kissed a complete stranger. "I'm going to call it a night."

"Yes, ma'am. I think that's a good idea," he murmured, and took the margarita glass from her trembling fingers. "Shall I walk you to your room?"

For one wild, crazy second, she was sure his words were code for *Can I spend the night doing decadent, indecent things to you?* In the next instant, she dismissed the thought, as alluring as it was. She'd misread his intent to kiss her, so she was no doubt imagining the suggestion in his voice, too.

"No, thanks," she replied. "I know the way."

Was it just wishful thinking, or did he actually look disappointed?

"Okay, then. Sleep well," he said.

Yeah, right. Like there was any chance of that happening.

With as much composure as she could muster, she walked toward the house. Once inside, she practically sprinted up the staircase. Inside her room, she shed the borrowed T-shirt and bottoms, balled them up and hurled them into a far corner. She had no idea what she was going to wear tomorrow, but she'd be damned if she'd put those hideous clothes back on her body.

Then, clad in nothing but her panties, she shut the light off and edged under the cool bedsheets, leaving her midriff uncovered. A warm breeze wafted in through the open windows and caressed her skin, taunting her. With a groan, she turned on her side, dragged the covers up over her shoulders and determinedly closed her eyes.

"Sleep well." Ha. She'd be lucky if she got any sleep, especially when all she could think about were hazel eyes and a pair of lips so temptingly sinful that she still ached at their loss.

IT WAS ALMOST TWO O'CLOCK in the morning when Ivy finally gave up any pretense of sleeping. Aside from the margarita she'd had earlier that night, she hadn't eaten anything since she'd left New York, and she was starving.

But it wasn't her stomach that kept her awake. It was the absolute stillness surrounding the hacienda. She'd lived in New York City the past five years, and the constant hum of traffic and wail of sirens had become comforting background noises that helped lull her to sleep. Even the streets of Montreal, which were quiet in comparison with New York City's, had had their buzz. Out here, however, in the remote mountains of Mexico, the silence was almost unbearable.

An image of Garrett drifted through her mind. Was he asleep? Had he thought of her after she'd left the pool area? Had he seen how much she'd wanted him?

With a despairing huff, she threw aside the covers and swung her legs over the side of the bed. The room suddenly felt overly warm, suffocating. Even the ceiling fan circulating the air did little to cool her heated flesh. She was restless with need. She couldn't get his image out of her head, and the Technicolor fantasies she'd had about him earlier had only made her more hot and bothered. It was crazy, but the guy completely distracted her. Made her think about doing things she hadn't done with any man in a long time. Too long, in fact.

She enjoyed sex. She *wanted* sex. Good sex. She had the distinct feeling that sex with Garrett Stokes wouldn't just be good but totally off-the-charts amazing.

Sitting up, she scooped her hair off her neck, wishing she'd turned on the air-conditioning before getting into bed. She'd figured open windows would be more comfortable than the climate control, but she'd been wrong. A sheen of sweat covered her skin.

She switched on the bedside lamp and then padded across the room to flip on the air-conditioning. Crossing to the casement windows, she pulled them closed and thought longingly of the swimming pool and its cool, blue depths. The pool seemed the perfect antidote to her current ailment, and at this hour she was unlikely to encounter anybody.

Grateful that she'd packed her bathing suits in the smaller suitcase, she donned a simple one-piece suit and a terry-cloth robe. After retrieving a bottle of water from the small fridge, she crept down the hallway, past the closed doors of the other rooms. She wondered which room belonged to Garrett. The last thing she needed was to run into him.

She hastily suppressed a snort of laughter at the thought. Given her frustrated state, *she'd* probably attack *him*. As soon as she stepped outside, she drew in a thankful breath, inhaling the heady fragrance of hibiscus and mango blossoms. The humidity had dissipated somewhat and the temperature was cooler than it had been in her bedroom.

Despite the fact that silence had kept her awake, she

realized the night was far from quiet. She stood for a moment on the walkway and listened. The sound of crickets was everywhere, interspersed with the occasional hoot of a night owl and the distant scream of something Ivy didn't want to think about. Fireflies dotted the darkness, their blinking lights like a reflection of the overhead stars. Tilting her head back, she studied them. She had never seen stars like this in New York City. They were brilliant, and so abundant, as if some careless hand had strewn billions of diamonds across the sky.

She followed the tiled pathway through the central courtyard and around the side of the hacienda to the pool area. The patio lights had been turned off, but the lights in the pool were on, softly illuminating the water.

Ivy let her robe drop to the ground, then stood at the edge of the deep end and dove cleanly into the water. She stroked underwater to the shallow end and came up with a satisfied gasp—only to find herself staring at a pair of masculine legs.

Naked masculine legs.

Swiping water out of her eyes, she followed their length upward and saw with shock that they were attached to a very naked Eric Terrell. He held a drink in one hand and swayed as he leered down at her.

Where had he come from? Glancing around the pool area, she spotted a robe draped over a chaise partially concealed behind a cluster of potted palms. *Damn.* Why hadn't she looked more closely?

"Ivy James," he said, his voice slurred, "so nice to see you again."

Ivy quickly averted her gaze, although she'd gotten enough of an eyeful to realize he was probably too inebriated to do much more than leer.

"Eric," she replied in a strangled voice. She pushed herself back into the water and glided to another wall of the pool. "I wasn't expecting anyone out here at this time of night. Um, where are your clothes?"

He laughed as if delighted she'd noticed. "Well, I guess I wasn't expectin' to see anyone out here, either." He strolled over to where she clung to the side of the pool. "But now that you're here…be a shame to let this go to waste." He waggled his hips suggestively, as if unaware that his body wasn't quite up to the task he envisioned it for.

Ivy laughed uncertainly. Inwardly, she cursed. How had she managed to get herself into such an awkward situation? The guy had no business coming on to her in such a crude way, but, damn it, he was Eric-Freaking-Terrell. She couldn't just tell him where to stick it. Not if she expected to keep her job.

"Ah, thanks, but I'll have to pass."

When it seemed he might actually lean down and offer her a hand, Ivy pushed herself back into the water and swam to the far side of the pool. Unfortunately, the only way back to the hacienda was past him. Once again she realized that in his intoxicated state, he wasn't actually a threat, but neither did she want to play games. She couldn't imagine anything more undignified than being chased around a swimming pool by a naked, drunken Eric Terrell.

He took a hefty swig of his drink as he considered her. "Well, then," he finally said, moving with the studied precision of somebody who'd consumed way too much alcohol. "I'm just going to have to come in there and change your mind."

A masculine voice cleared itself behind Eric, startling him so that he staggered and sloshed the contents of his glass over his hand. "Goddamn it, Stokes, don't you know better 'n to sneak up behind someone like that?"

Garrett Stokes materialized from the shadows, his eyes going straight to Ivy. Even from this distance, she could read the question there. *You okay?* She gave a barely perceptible nod.

He carried a towel in one hand, and now he thrust it at Eric. "Hey, man, cover up. There's a lady present."

"I can see that," Eric said, scowling at Garrett. "You're interruptin' my efforts to get to know her better."

"Say good-night, champ. Ivy's here to meet me, so you'll have to find yourself another girl." He pressed the towel into Eric's chest until the other man had no choice but to take it.

Eric stared first at Garrett, then at Ivy. "That right? You're together?"

"That's right."

"Shit."

Garrett walked around the pool to Ivy, reached down and offered her a hand. She gasped as he hauled her effortlessly out of the water, but she wasn't prepared when he wrapped an arm around her shoulders and tucked her against his side, heedless that she was dripping water all over him. "C'mon, babe, let's get you out of that wet suit."

He shot her a meaningful look, and Ivy's acting skills kicked into gear. "The sooner, the better," she said in a sultry tone, and stood on tiptoe to plant a moist kiss against his jaw. She felt him stiffen, but he recovered swiftly.

"I already ran you a bath," he replied, and drew her along with him as he circled the pool. "Eric, have a good night."

Eric had wrapped the towel around his hips, and now he raised his glass in a mock salute. "G'night, kids. Be good," he said, the words slurred. "And if you can't be good, be careful."

Ivy and Garrett made their way back toward the hacienda, but he didn't withdraw his arm from around her shoulders.

"Cold?" he asked.

She shook her head, too dismayed by this turn of events to answer. He was too close. Too completely irresistible. Her heightened senses absorbed everything. The warmth from his body seeped through the wet fabric of her bathing suit as his thumb soothed a circular pattern on her bare shoulder. He probably wasn't even aware he was doing it. He smelled incredible, of clean soap and citrus.

They entered the dim interior of the hacienda, and at the foot of the winding stairs, she pulled him to a stop. "I'll be okay from here."

"If you don't mind, I'd just as soon walk you to your door."

There'd be no arguing with him—she could see that from the implacable expression in his eyes. She nodded and tucked a wet strand of hair behind her ear. "Sure. Okay."

He released her, and they slowly climbed the stairs.

"Thanks for—for intervening the way you did," she said when they reached the top. "Did you know we were out there, or was it just luck?"

One black eyebrow arched upward, and Ivy realized that nothing this guy did was a result of luck.

"I saw you walk out to the pool," he said, confirming her suspicion. "Somebody should have warned you that Eric's a night owl. If we were in a city, he'd be at a club, surrounded by women happy to give him all the attention he wanted. Even here, there're usually a few girls hanging around the pool in the hope he'll make a late-night appearance."

They'd arrived at her room, and she faced him, uncertain what to do. Would he expect her to invite him in? Or would he simply say goodbye? He was so close that one small step would bring her smack up against the hard planes of his muscled chest. Every nerve in her body tingled with awareness, and she forgot to breathe as their eyes locked.

His shimmered, hot and bright, and an answering heat unfurled low in her center. It spread outward until every cell in her body urged her to step forward and press herself wantonly against him. She couldn't remember the last time she'd had such an immediate, raw reaction to a man.

"Well, I'm confident I could have handled him if he'd gotten frisky," she responded, forcing herself to think rationally, "but I'm glad I didn't have to. It would have made working with him so awkward."

"He probably won't even recall it in the morning," Garrett assured her. His eyes lingered on her face, then dropped slowly to her breasts. His voice roughened. "You're cold. You should go in."

Following his gaze, Ivy saw her nipples were hard nubs beneath the thin material of her bathing suit. But only she knew it had nothing to do with the damp fabric and everything to do with his proximity. Just the fact that his eyes were on her was enough for her body to tighten, and her nipples ripened even more.

"I forgot," she said in a husky voice, "that my room key is in the pocket of my robe."

Which she'd left at the pool.

Garrett reached into his back pocket, pulled out his wallet and flipped it open, but before she could see what he intended to do, he turned away from her, shielding the wallet from her view. What might she have seen? A photo? A condom, maybe? *Be Prepared.* Wasn't that the army motto? Or was it the Boy Scout motto? She couldn't think clearly.

When he turned back to her, he held the closed wallet in one hand and a credit card in the other. "Don't let housekeeping know I did this," he said, and edged the card into the doorjamb beside the keyhole. All it took was several deft movements and the door clicked open.

"Wow," she murmured approvingly. "A man of many talents."

"Yes, ma'am," he agreed silkily, his voice rich with meaning. "And you don't know the half of it."

His words caused her imagination to flame, and she had an almost overwhelming urge to drag him into her room so he could demonstrate just how talented he might be.

He braced on arm against the wall as she leaned back against the door with one hand on the knob and stared up at him. A bar of light slanted through the partially open door and cast intriguing shadows over his face and body. Ivy's gaze drifted down his body to where his T-shirt clung damply to his chest.

"You're wet," she observed softly.

"So are you." His voice was languid, his smile lazy. *You don't know the half of it.*

"You're different than I expected," she said, smiling.

"Oh, yeah? How's that?"

Ivy shrugged. "I don't know. More easygoing. I thought all you military types were total hard-asses."

Garrett smiled, and it completely transformed his face. "I guess it all depends on the situation."

Mesmerized by his smile and the way his eyes crinkled at the corners, Ivy needed a full second to collect herself.

"I should probably get some sleep." But she didn't move, just continued to stare at him.

He wasn't smiling now. He swallowed hard, and his gaze fell to her mouth.

Stepping forward, Ivy placed her hands lightly against his chest and brushed her lips sweetly over his. "Thank you," she whispered.

The kiss was meant to be a nice one, a closed-mouth one that conveyed her thanks and appreciation. But the moment their lips met, heat flared. With a groan of surrender, Garrett captured her face between his big hands and slanted his mouth boldly across hers. She didn't resist when she felt his tongue against hers, and then there was only fierce need that made her nipples ache and her center throb.

The kiss was everything she wanted, and more. Ivy wound her arms around his neck, speared her fingers through his hair and reveled in the hard, solid feel of him flush against her from chest to knees. He slid a hand to the base of her spine and pressed her forward so that she could feel his growing erection beneath his jeans.

When he dragged his mouth from hers, she actually whimpered in disappointment. He lowered his lips to her neck and gently bit the tender flesh, causing shivers of sensation.

At that moment, a door opened farther along the corridor and the sound of female voices drifted toward them. They came closer, and Ivy closed her eyes, aware that she and Garrett were still plastered together in her doorway, with her wearing next to nothing. Two women sauntered past, wineglasses in their hands and knowing smiles on their faces. They spoke in hushed tones, but Ivy heard them just the same.

"…Ivy James, the new girl…sleeps with all her leading men…she's sure not wasting any time…"

When the women were gone, Ivy stepped away from Garrett. Without looking at him, she smoothed the front of his T-shirt with her hands, feeling the thump of his heart beneath her fingers.

"I—I should go in," she murmured.

"Ivy—"

"Good night, Garrett."

"*Wait.*"

His voice was low, but insistent. Reluctantly, Ivy gazed at him, and her chest tightened at the understanding reflected in his eyes.

"Don't say anything," she pleaded softly. "It doesn't matter."

"It matters to me," he said grimly. "I'm the one who put you in a compromising position." He raked a hand through his hair. "I'm just sorry you had to hear that."

Ivy gave him a lopsided smile. "Why? It's not entirely untrue."

"That's irrelevant. Your personal life is your own business. If you want, I can speak to them."

Ivy swallowed hard against the unexpected lump in her throat. He wasn't judging her. If anything, he seemed ready to go to battle for her.

"No, but thanks. It's not necessary." She gave him a reassuring smile. "I, um, should really go in. Good night."

Without giving him an opportunity to dissuade her, and before she could do something completely rash, like drag him with her through the doorway, she slipped into her room and closed the door firmly behind her.

She leaned back against it for a moment, until she heard Garrett move away. Only then did she throw the dead bolt and slide the chain into place, before stripping out of her soggy swimsuit. The air-conditioning had done its job, and the air was chilly against her naked flesh.

She wouldn't let the bitchy remarks she'd overheard get to her. She hadn't slept with *all* her leading men, and technically speaking, Garrett Stokes didn't even fall into that category.

But despite his assurances that her personal life was her own business, she didn't want him thinking less of her. It was important to her that he understood she wasn't a woman who went casually into relationships. She'd been in love with each of the men she'd become involved with during the filming of her previous films. At least, at the time, she'd believed herself to be in love with them. That had to count for something, right?

Shivering, she snatched a towel from the bathroom and vigorously toweled her wet hair until it began to dry in springy curls around her face. It would look like hell tomorrow, but she didn't care.

She slid beneath the blankets and switched off the bedside lamp then groaned and thumped her pillow in frustration. *Damn, damn, damn.* What was wrong with her? She didn't know what she regretted most—letting Garrett, a near-perfect stranger, kiss her so thoroughly, or letting him leave before he could finish what they'd begun.

4

It was all Ivy could do not to twist her face away from the passionate kiss, especially when Eric's slick tongue insinuated itself between her lips. She fought the urge to bite down on it, and instead arched against him and forced her arms to encircle his neck and stroke his shoulders in a parody of sexual need. Inwardly, she fumed with outrage.

They'd been trying to shoot this particular love scene for more than two hours, but couldn't seem to get it right. They'd done seventeen takes, and each time something had gone wrong. Either the lights hadn't faded properly, or the camera movement had been wrong or, as with the last several takes, Eric had forgotten his lines.

Ivy was beginning to suspect he had done so deliberately.

Again she acknowledged there were women out there who would kill to be in her position. Literally. Less than a week ago, she'd been starry-eyed at the prospect of being cast as Eric Terrell's love interest, but it hadn't taken her long to realize the fantasy she'd woven was a far cry from reality.

Her mouth felt bruised from being crushed against his, and she knew her lips must look swollen and chapped from his kisses. But what infuriated her most was how he used the scene as an excuse to touch her more intimately than the script required. Maybe he figured he was helping her get into character, but instead she found his groping jarred her out of the scene.

Beneath the threadbare sheet of the narrow bed, she wore nothing but a beige-colored thong. Eric, clad in a pair of minuscule briefs, was positioned between her thighs. Finn had directed Eric to support himself above her on one elbow and use his free hand to stroke her face and neck and those parts of her body that weren't hidden. But at one point, he'd run his hand under the sheet and briefly cupped her breast, even lightly pinching her nipple, so that she'd yelped in surprise. The scene had been cut.

Apart from that one squeal of surprise, she hadn't said anything to Eric. She'd been too acutely conscious of Garrett Stokes, standing just behind the cameras, watching her performance. She wouldn't let him or any of the other crew members know how much Eric's action bothered her. They'd think she was inexperienced and a prude, and they'd be partly right. The truth was, she'd never felt so out of her element as she did with this project. No matter how she tried, she just couldn't relax enough to slide into Helena Vanderveer's skin.

Despite Finn's skillful directing and his unfailing courtesy, she knew she was testing his patience. Once, he'd even suggested that perhaps she was uncomfortable doing the love scene, but she'd disagreed. She'd done partially nude love scenes. Her discomfort wasn't from the knowledge that a dozen or more of the crew, including camera operators, gaffers and dolly grips, stood on the sidelines, observing.

It had nothing to do with her confidence, or the

script, or even Eric Terrell, who was slyly going in for another grope.

It had everything to do with the man just out of her line of vision. His sharp, predatory eyes missed nothing, and without having to look, she could feel him watching her.

In the scene where Helena and Garrett first make love, the script had called for her to undress slowly, almost shyly, before inching into the small bed beside Eric. Just the awareness that Garrett Stokes's eyes were on her had been enough to cause a hot tide of color to wash into her face, and she hadn't had to feign the shyness that had swept over her as her blouse and bra had slid to the floor.

Finn had been elated with that particular take, saying she'd performed flawlessly. When Ivy had reluctantly glanced toward the area where Garrett stood, the surrounding shadows had concealed his expression, but she couldn't help wondering what he'd thought of the take. Of her. Did he consider her performance flawless? Did he find her attractive? How did she compare with the real Helena Vanderveer? The endless questions plagued her, even as she tried to concentrate on her work.

They'd begun shooting three days earlier, starting with the scenes where Helena discovers the injured soldier in the jungle behind the mission and brings him to a room hidden beneath the floor of the small chapel. The set dressers had completely altered the room to resemble a tiny cellar chamber, containing a bed, a chair, a washstand and little else. In this chamber Garrett and Helena fall in love, transforming the dark, dingy surroundings into an intimate hideaway for their blossoming passion.

In full makeup and costume, Eric had been almost unrecognizable. He looked tough and dangerous. The special-effects team had done an amazing job of creating realistic injuries on his flawless body, and he'd assumed the persona of a hardened soldier with seemingly little effort.

Now here she was, pressed against him from knee to chin, his lips feasting on hers, and all she could think about was another pair of lips, more tempting even than Eric's. Her hands stroked over Eric's shoulders, encountered his cropped golden hair, and all she could think of was running her fingers through hair that was longer and darker.

Sweet Mary, what was wrong with her? Every woman in America had fantasized about being with this guy, and here she was, thinking about somebody else. Now, as his hand trailed along her rib cage, he captured her mouth in another deep kiss. At the same time, he nudged her thighs farther apart and settled himself more comfortably in the cradle of her hips. She could feel him hard and erect, pressing against her most intimate parts. She had to force herself to remain still and not shove him off her.

Eric Terrell had been right about one thing—he *really* got into his character. If not for the fragile barrier of her panties, she had no doubt he'd be trying to get into *her*, with or without the film crew looking on.

Ivy kept her eyes shut and told herself to just go with it; this was what two people lost in the throes of passion *would* do. But when he shoved his tongue deep into her mouth and simultaneously closed one hand around her breast, she forgot about the filming and responded instinctively, tearing her mouth away and shoving him hard enough that he lost his balance and sprawled gracelessly on top of her with a loud curse.

"Cut!"

Finn MacDougall barked the word with all the energy and disgust of an army drill sergeant who'd just realized his new recruits were better suited to beauty school than boot camp.

Mortified that she'd just ruined another take, Ivy twisted her face to one side and pushed at Eric's shoulders until he rolled away and flopped onto his back, one arm flung wearily over his eyes.

Conscious of the others who watched her from behind the cameras, Ivy dragged the threadbare sheet over her nakedness and scooted back on the thin mattress until her shoulders were up against the cold stone wall. She felt ill not just from Eric's unwelcome groping but because she'd probably just destroyed any chance of hanging on to her part. Finn would replace her, and she couldn't blame him.

He emerged from behind the main camera and strode across the dirt floor of the small set toward the bed. He wasn't a classically handsome man—his nose was too prominent and his eyes too deep set. But he had a compelling presence that drew attention wherever he went. Now his bushy eyebrows were drawn together, and his lips were compressed in a thin line.

He stood beside the bed, hands on his hips as his gaze moved between Eric and Ivy. "Look, maybe we should call it a day and go back to this scene tomorrow."

Eric withdrew his arm from his eyes and propped himself up on one elbow. "No way," he countered. "I want to get this scene done today."

"Eric, you can't even remember your lines," Finn said, exasperation edging his voice. "You're both tired, and quite frankly, I'm just not feeling any chemistry between the two of you."

Eric glared at Ivy accusingly. "Yeah, well, if Miss Frigid over here would relax—"

Ivy gasped and clutched the sheet tighter. "Oh, please, give me a break! This is supposed to be a love scene, not a rape scene." She eyed Finn imploringly, her voice filled with indignation. "He grabbed my *breast*. I'm pretty sure that wasn't in the script."

"It's called improvisation," Eric snarled. "If you had any experience with *real* films, you'd understand that sometimes you just need to go with your instincts."

Before she could respond, Garrett Stokes was there, leaning over her to stick one hard finger into Eric's chest. Ivy stared in utter fascination at his face, scant inches above her own. His eyes darkened as he glowered at the startled actor, and a muscle worked convulsively in his lean jaw. He spoke through gritted teeth in a deceptively low voice.

"How about I go with *my* instincts?" he ground out, using his finger to push Eric back against the cold wall. "You so much as breathe in a way that isn't written in that script, you so much as *look* at her in a way that makes her uncomfortable, and I'll be all over you like stink on shit." He gave the actor a shove. "You got that?"

Eric glowered back at him for several seconds, and Ivy had an insane, completely inappropriate urge to giggle at the very real fear that flashed in Eric's eyes. Then he seemed to pull himself together before he yanked Garrett's hand away and sat up.

"Yeah, I got it," he muttered, a dark flush staining his neck. "But let me tell you this. Your little missionary here needs to loosen up." His lips curled in a sneer. "Maybe you want to give her another reminder of just what it was you shared with Helena while she was nursing you back to health."

"Maybe I should give you a reminder—"

"Okay, okay, you both made your point." Finn laid a hand on Garrett's arm, interrupting his snarled response, and the other man reluctantly straightened. Finn impaled Garrett with a meaningful look. "We'll talk about this later."

Garrett blew out his breath and raked a hand through his hair, but not before he pinioned Eric with one last glare. "Yeah, we will." He gazed down at Ivy and his expression softened, if only slightly. "You okay?"

She nodded mutely and watched as he returned to the side of the set, rubbing the back of his neck.

She recalled his earlier words about how every woman responded differently to a man's touch. Okay, so she definitely had *not* responded to Eric's caresses the way she'd responded to Garrett's, but she knew from their brief encounter that Garrett would employ a little more finesse in his lovemaking than Eric would.

Recalling the intense expression in Garrett's eyes as he'd intervened, she felt a delicious shiver run through her. She couldn't believe he'd confronted Eric the way he had. When was the last time a guy had done something so chivalrous for her? Aside from the night Garrett had rescued her from Eric's drunken attentions, she couldn't ever remember such gallantry. His intervention moments ago made her feel both feminine and fragile that he'd been concerned for her well-being. For just an instant, her imagination surged. What she wouldn't give to have Garrett play himself! She definitely wouldn't have to fake an orgasm.

"Okay, listen up," Finn was saying to the rest of the crew. "That's a wrap. We could shoot this scene a dozen—a hundred—more times and it wouldn't do any good." He nodded at Eric. "Go ahead and hit the showers. I've decided not to film the love scenes until next week. Tomorrow, we'll head out to Xalapa and wrap up the remaining jungle scenes with the drug cartel." His gaze shifted back to Ivy. "You need to take a few days off and give this part some serious thought."

Ivy's mouth fell open. She was shocked and relieved that he wasn't kicking her off his set.

"No, listen to me," Finn said firmly, misunderstanding her expression. He lowered his voice so that the rest of the crew wouldn't overhear him. "I brought you onto this project with some reservations, but you came so highly recommended that I decided to offer you the role." His eyes flicked to Eric. "I don't know what's going on with either of you, but there's absolutely no chemistry here. In fact, there's so much animosity between the two of you that I feel like I'm watching a pro-wrestling match." He turned back to Ivy. "I know you can do this—I've seen your other films. So here's what I recommend. Take the next few days and do whatever you have to do to find some inspiration."

Ivy nodded her agreement, too grateful that he hadn't fired her to argue.

"Don't come back until you're ready to put everything you have into the love scenes and get them right." Finn's voice was hard. "Remember, Helena is hugely attracted to this soldier. She wants him. She's falling in love with him. She needs to communicate all this during their lovemaking, *not* shrink from him." He wagged a finger admonishingly at Ivy. "Now is not the time for your acting skills to go on vacation. Forget about the cameras. Women all over the world would kill to be in your place right now."

Ivy wanted to tell Finn that it wasn't the cameras she found so distracting, and that she'd gladly trade places with those other women if it meant she wouldn't have to get naked again with Eric Terrell. Instead, she just nodded anew.

"I want energy. I want *emotion*." Finn looked back and forth between the two of them, then pinned Eric with a glare. "And I don't want any more of the crap I saw today. It won't be tolerated on my set. Do I make myself clear?"

Eric nodded mutely, but Ivy didn't miss the resentful glance he shot her. As soon as Finn turned away and began directing the crew to break down the cameras, Eric stepped off the bed and snatched a dressing robe from his personal assistant, who hovered nervously nearby. He thrust his arms into the sleeves and belted the robe around his waist as he stared down at Ivy, who was still curled up beneath the sheet.

"Don't worry," he said, smiling in a way that set Ivy's teeth on edge. "If you're too squeamish to do the love scenes, we can always bring in a body double."

As if on cue, Denise, the makeup artist, stepped onto the set and handed Eric a cool drink. She pointedly ignored Ivy. Eric accepted the glass, then deliberately ran his gaze over the other woman's body with a practiced eye.

"Now that I think of it," he said musingly, "you and Denise have similar body types. In fact, without seeing your faces, a person could easily mistake one for the other. And I know for a fact that Denise has some…experience with love scenes." Then, smiling broadly, he tipped his glass at Ivy in a mock toast, before he turned and walked away, a bewildered and red-faced Denise close behind him.

Ivy narrowed her eyes at his retreating back. She couldn't say if he and the other woman were sleeping together, and she didn't particularly care. Denise was welcome to him. But Ivy did wonder if his threat had any substance. Finn wouldn't really consider substituting a body double for the love scenes, would he? There *were* actors who flatly refused to do nude scenes, forcing a director to either dispense with the nudity or bring in a body double. But she wasn't one of those actors. She was experienced, a professional. She just had to put her personal feelings aside and get on with it.

"Hey. You sure you're okay?"

Glancing up, she saw Garrett standing over the bed holding her dressing robe. He watched her in a way that made her feel as vulnerable and helpless as a kitten. His entire stance was protective, as if he was her very own bodyguard and heaven help anyone who tried to mess with her.

"Yes," she said, summoning a smile. "I'm fine." She took the robe from him and drew it on, careful to keep the sheet in place until she'd secured the sash. "So I guess you'll be going into the jungle with Finn and the crew, huh?"

"Actually, I'm going to hang around here for a couple of days," he responded. "Finn and I already went over the scenes with the drug cartel, and he doesn't need me on location for those shoots." He smiled wryly. "The terrain is pretty rough. I'd just slow them down."

Somehow, Ivy doubted it. Even with his bad leg, she was pretty sure there wasn't much he couldn't do. The guy oozed capability.

Finn called his name, and Ivy observed Garrett as he consulted a map with the director. She couldn't help but admire Garrett's physical grace. He stood with his head slightly bent, one thumb hooked in the front pocket of his pants as he nodded at something Finn said. His black hair fell back from his square forehead in loose waves. He wore a faded T-shirt that was frayed at the hem and a pair of jeans that hugged his trim backside and emphasized the length of his legs. The strong muscles of his back and shoulders were evident through the thin material of the shirt, and again Ivy wondered what it would be like to run her hands over all that firmness.

Eric Terrell, still clad in his bathrobe, moved to stand on Finn's other side. His handsome face had graced the cover of countless magazines; his name was synonymous with sex appeal. Yet when compared with Garrett Stokes, he was like a green recruit. Garrett was the real deal, and he looked every inch of it.

Dark. Dangerous. Compelling. And sexy as hell.

Ivy climbed off the bed, still watching the two men, and suddenly, she knew what she had to do. In order to portray her character realistically, she had to learn everything she could about Helena Vanderveer, especially what had happened between her and Garrett. She had the script to go by, but it was too superficial for her to gain an in-depth understanding of Helena's character. She wanted to get into the missionary's head, discover what it was that had compelled the woman to sleep with Garrett Stokes after knowing him for so short a time.

What had made Helena risk her life for a man who, despite their intimacies, was a virtual stranger? Although really, looking at the guy, Ivy had a pretty good idea what had driven Helena to act as she had. Garrett Stokes was the embodiment of everything sexy and masculine. He was a true-life hero, a guy who would risk everything for what he believed in. A woman would have to be crazy to let a man like him go.

While Ivy would have preferred to talk to Helena Vanderveer herself about her experiences, that was clearly out of the question. But asking Garrett Stokes to give her details wasn't. And not just for pointers. For the whole shebang.

5

GARRETT LAY IN A ROPE hammock beside the *casita* he'd claimed as his own, enjoying the darkness and listening to the night bugs in the trees. He cradled a cold beer in one hand and idly pushed the hammock into a gentle swing with one bare foot on the ground. In his other hand, he held a photo. He'd pulled it out of his wallet hours ago, and despite the fact the sun had set and he could no longer see the image, he hadn't put the photo away. He smoothed his thumb across the snapshot, feeling the familiar creases from where it had been folded and tucked into his wallet so many times.

It was a picture of Ivy, taken several years earlier. If he closed his eyes, he could see the image in his mind. A younger Ivy, laughing into the camera, a hand lifted to capture the errant corkscrew of hair that had blown across her cheek. She was at the beach, and he could just make out the sweep of ocean in the blurred background. The shot wasn't a posed one, like the promotional photos she'd done for the release of her films. It wasn't a paparazzo photo, either, taken without her consent or knowledge. It was a joyful candid, captured by someone she'd trusted. Garrett didn't know for certain, but he suspected her brother, Devon, had snapped it.

Garrett had carried the photo with him since shortly after Devon James had died. Once the doctors had declared him dead, Ivy had briefly been allowed back into the small hospital room. Garrett knew she had no memory of the soldier who'd occupied the narrow hospital bed next to her brother's, and why would she? The curtain between the beds had been open enough for her to see him, but his head had been bandaged and his face swollen and discolored to the point where his own mother would have had difficulty recognizing him.

Through a medicated haze, he'd watched her weep before carefully placing the photo on the blanket that covered Devon. Garrett must have made a sound, because for one instant, she'd looked over at him. In that split second, his entire world had shifted.

Her departure had caused a rush of air to billow over the bed, and the photograph had fluttered from its resting place and drifted to the floor beneath Garrett's bed. Several days had passed before he'd been able to get a janitor to retrieve it for him. His promise to Devon aside, he'd had some half-baked fantasy that he'd find her and make her smile again, the way she did in the photo. After a while, the photo had become his motivation, the reason he'd endured the months of torturous rehabilitation necessary to his recovery.

It was stupid, he knew, but sometimes that photo had been the one thing that kept him going. He had told himself that once he was fully recovered, he'd look her up. He'd make sure she was doing okay, just as he'd promised her brother. Although Garrett had indeed followed her career, he'd never gotten up the courage to contact her. He'd told himself she was doing just fine, that she didn't need anyone watching over her. But he'd watched over her just the same, albeit from a distance. Their relationship probably never would have amounted to anything more than a distant infatuation.

But the day Finn had approached him about making a movie had changed that.

Even then, he hadn't set out to bring Ivy on board the project. But when he'd read the script and realized Finn had taken artistic license in portraying Helena Vanderveer as young and beautiful, he knew he wanted Ivy to have the role. He'd wanted—no, he'd *needed*—to know how she'd been since he'd first seen in her in that hospital room.

Nothing could have prepared him for the sight of Ivy James in the flesh. She had completely blown him away. As soon as he'd laid eyes on her, he'd known his attraction to her was more than just physical. Something in her eyes called to him. He'd never considered himself a romantic. He was a realist. He'd had absolutely no belief in love at first sight.

Until he had seen Ivy James.

Images of her swam behind his closed eyes. Slim. Pale. Naked.

He groaned and took a hefty swig of his beer. Not following her into her room the night she'd kissed him had required every ounce of self-restraint he had. Even now, he could feel the softness of her lips, the heat in her skin that the pool water hadn't managed to chill. She'd warmed up fast once he'd started kissing her back. He'd wanted to devour her.

The way he'd devoured her with his eyes during today's shoot. He'd watched, mesmerized, as she'd shyly removed her clothing for the first love scene. He hadn't been the only one on that set who'd sucked in his breath when her blouse had drifted to the dirt floor. Just about every guy in the room, excluding Finn, had let out a sigh of appreciation. She'd been luminous, and Garrett thought he'd never seen anything as erotic as her slender back, curving into the gentle swell of her hips. Her breasts were lush, with rosy nipples that practically begged to be touched.

He honestly didn't understand how the camera and lighting guys managed to concentrate on their jobs when such scenes unfolded in front of them. He'd had to swallow the hard knot of jealousy that had formed in his throat when she'd slid beneath the sheet to join Eric on the narrow bed.

He took another swig of beer, recalling the moment Eric's hand had closed over Ivy's breast. He'd been halfway across the set before one of the assistant directors had caught his arm to hold him back. He'd regained his self-control—but barely.

When he'd told Finn he wanted Ivy James to play the part of Helena, he'd known that some scenes would require her to get up close and personal with Eric Terrell. He just hadn't thought his own reaction would be so visceral. He'd wanted to annihilate the actor, drag him out of the bed and pummel his perfect, smug face until it was nothing but a bloody mess.

Disgusted with himself and how close he'd come to losing control, he drained the rest of the beer in one long swallow, then curled an arm behind his head and looked toward the hacienda. From his vantage point on the hammock, he could see the window of Ivy's room on the second floor. He'd chosen the room for her because of its location. Not only did it have a nice view of the mountains, but it also faced his cottage. Her lights had been out for about ten minutes.

He was idly conjuring up sultry images of her silken limbs entwined with the bedclothes—entwined around *him*—when a twig snapped somewhere in the darkness. It wasn't much of a sound, but his senses went on alert.

He continued to gently push the hammock with one foot, while his eyes sought the shadows just beyond the perimeter of the cottage.

He stopped breathing.

He watched, intrigued, as Ivy James materialized from the gloom and crept toward the screened door of the *casita*. The hammock was a good twenty feet from the cabin, strung between two lush breadnut trees. In the unrelenting darkness, she didn't see him. She raised a hand to knock on the door, then hesitated, apparently having second thoughts. Her hand fisted, then fell to her side. She was going to leave.

Garrett cleared his throat.

"Oh!" Startled, she whirled in his direction, her hand flying to her throat as her eyes searched the darkness. "Garrett?"

He refolded the snapshot, tucked it back into his wallet, then swung his other leg to the ground. Standing to ease the stiffness in his bad leg, he pushed the wallet into the back pocket of his jeans. "Yeah, it's me." He walked toward her. "What are you doing out here?"

As he moved closer, the pale blur of her face shifted into focus. Her eyes were pools of black. She wore some kind of little dress that left her arms and legs bare, and her thick hair was pulled into a ponytail.

"I—I wanted to talk to you."

Interesting.

"Oh, yeah? What about?"

She glanced uneasily toward the dense woods behind him and hugged her arms around her middle. "Do we have to stand out here, in the dark? Could we go inside and maybe turn on a light?"

He shrugged, his mind furiously working through all the reasons she might be there. At his door. After dark.

"Sure."

Reaching over, he opened the screen door. It groaned on its ancient hinges. As she brushed past him, he caught the scent of something heady. Jasmine, maybe.

He followed her into the cabin and took down a kerosene lantern from a hook. Ivy stepped out of his way and waited quietly while he set the lantern on a nearby table, adjusted the wick, then lit it with a long match that he drew from a tin box. The bright flame created a warm glow, chasing away the shadows that surrounded them and casting golden light across her features.

He could see Ivy's sleeveless dress was pale green, cinched at the waist with a narrow belt. It looked like some retro style from the 1950s. It should have made her resemble Beaver Cleaver's mother, but Garrett found the dress incredibly alluring simply because Ivy was the one wearing it. The top several buttons were undone, revealing the smooth skin beneath and her fragile collarbone.

He wanted badly to touch her.

Instead, he pushed aside a wooden bowl filled with fresh limes, shoved the lantern to the center of the rough-hewn table, perched one hip on the edge and waited.

Clearly uncomfortable, Ivy stood in the center of the room and gazed around, her eyes moving over every-thing except him. She took in the gnarled, wooden shelves against one wall that housed his small collec-tion of books, his clothing and his toiletries. She barely glanced at the Coleman cooler under the window, where he stored his beer and bottled water, but her eyes absorbed every detail of his bed.

It consisted of a carved wooden frame and a mattress,

and was pushed against the wall and heaped with
bedding and pillows brought over from the hacienda.
Gossamer mosquito netting, suspended from the ceiling
rafter, enveloped the bed. Oh, yeah, he definitely wanted
to show her his bed, but he was pretty sure—despite the
kiss they'd shared—that she hadn't come out to his
cottage for *that*.

"Wow. This is—"

"Primitive. I know."

She smiled at him, a swift curving of her lips. "I was
going to say *cozy*."

Garrett shrugged. At Finn's request, the set department had done a great job of transforming the tiny
interior into an inviting, Spanish-themed retreat. Even
the brightly patterned rug that covered the unvarnished
floorboards was inviting. Not that it particularly
mattered to him. He didn't actually spend much time
there, except to sleep.

But with Ivy standing scant feet away and her fragrance filling his head, he was suddenly glad she found
the cottage appealing. Which prompted another
thought: *What the hell was she doing here?*

He crossed his arms over his chest. "So what brings
you out here?"

He noted with interest the flush that stained her neck
and crept upward until even the tips of her ears were red.
She twisted her fingers together, then drew in a deep
breath and—finally—looked straight at him.

"It's about today's shoot." She gestured helplessly.
"It was pretty bad."

Bad didn't even begin to describe it, Garrett noted
grimly. Apart from the enchantment of seeing Ivy
undress, the scene had had all the appeal of a poorly
acted, low-budget porn film. It was clear to anyone

watching just how much Ivy had disliked being skin-to-skin with Eric Terrell. Even before Eric had begun groping her beneath the sheet, Ivy's responses had been forced and mechanical.

Finn had been right. There'd been zero chemistry between them. Personally, Garrett had been okay with that. Totally okay. But professionally, he knew that if things didn't change, Finn could very well send Ivy packing. He had too much riding on the film to let one actor ruin it.

One of the reasons Finn had agreed to bring Ivy on board was that her love scenes were usually so realistic. She had an ability to bring a depth to her on-screen relationships that was both realistic and moving. That Ivy had been involved with each of her on-screen love interests no doubt played a huge part in making those scenes so believable—something Garrett preferred not to think about.

But today's shoot had completely lacked emotion. Still, there was no way Garrett was walking into the trap Ivy had laid. If she thought he was going to agree with her about the disastrous shoot, she was dead wrong.

He shrugged noncommittally.

She made a small sound of exasperation and tucked a loose tendril of hair behind her ear. "Oh, please. You don't have to pretend on my account. You were there. You saw the shoot. I mean, did it come even close to what you shared with Helena Vanderveer?"

Garrett stilled. He'd lied to Ivy that first day about his relationship with the missionary, and while he didn't typically spend time analyzing his past actions, this particular untruth had been eating at him. He wasn't even sure what devil had prompted him to tell Ivy the script was true to life. Only afterward did he acknowledge that he'd wanted to get under her skin.

The way she'd gotten under his.

He'd wanted to arouse her awareness of him, even though the little white lie implied he'd been involved with another woman. The truth was, he'd been more than half in love with Ivy ever since the day he had first seen her at Walter Reed Army Medical Center, even if she had no memory of his being there.

He'd watched every one of her films, and had followed her blossoming career during the past two years. He'd even used his USASOC—U.S. Army Special Operations Command—connections to run a check on her and determine if there was anyone significant in her life.

He knew she'd been involved with a couple of her costars, although none of the relationships had lasted much beyond the time it had taken to film the movie. Garrett tried to tell himself it didn't matter; her personal entanglements were her own business. But he knew he was only kidding himself. She was the sole reason he'd even agreed to let Finn make the damn movie, and just the thought of her with another guy caused his gut to tighten.

The earnestness of her question caused him a pang of guilt, and part of him wanted to fess up. He determinedly ignored it. "No," he finally answered. "It didn't even come close to what I shared with Helena." That, at least, was the truth.

Her face fell and her entire body seemed to sag. "I thought as much." She bent her head and wearily rubbed her eyes.

Garrett pushed himself away from the table and moved to stand directly in front of her. He used one hand to tip her chin, studying her. The defeat in her dark eyes almost undid him. "Hey," he at last managed to say. "It wasn't as bad as all that."

She gave a disbelieving huff and turned her face aside. "Yes, it was. It was…terrible." She avoided his eyes, focusing on her hands, instead. "Do you remember what you said to me that first day, about giving me pointers?"

Garrett felt his heartbeat falter. "Sure," he replied cautiously. "I remember."

Ivy drew in a deep breath and her voice dropped. "I—I need to ask you…"

She let the sentence trail off, as if unable to finish it. Garrett dipped his head to look into her eyes. "Yes?"

She straightened, drawing her shoulders back and meeting his gaze without flinching. "Well, I was hoping you could give me some pointers." She gestured helplessly. "With the love scenes."

Garrett had spent a lot of years in covert ops, and he'd seen and done things that would make even the strongest of men fold, but nothing had ever made him go as weak in the knees as Ivy's words did. For a moment, he couldn't even formulate a response.

When he'd said he'd be available to give her pointers, he'd never—even in his wildest dreams—imagined she'd actually need them. But if there was one thing Garrett had learned during his years in the military, it was to recognize a strategic opportunity and take full advantage of it. In this case, that wasn't something he was overly proud of. But he was willing to resort to subterfuge, he wanted her that much.

"I don't know." He injected a note of doubt into his voice. "Maybe. It depends. What exactly do you want to know?"

Ivy stared at him for a full moment, and it was all Garrett could do to maintain an expression of polite interest and not squirm beneath her scrutiny.

Her gaze traveled slowly over his features before finally lingering on his mouth.

When she spoke at last, her voice was so low he had to strain to hear it. "I want to know what attracted you to each other. I want to know how it was between the two of you. The looks you gave each other, the way she touched you. I—I want to know what the sex was like, and what made it so special. I want to know all the nuances of your relationship." She hesitated a moment. "I want to know everything."

IVY WATCHED AS GARRETT'S eyes darkened and his face grew taut. He was going to refuse her; she just knew it. Coming here had been a mistake, but she'd been desperate.

She had three days—four at most—to capture the essence of what Helena Vanderveer had experienced with Garrett Stokes. What Ivy had failed to consider was Garrett's own feelings on the matter. For all Ivy knew, he and the missionary were still in love. That Ivy had shared one hot kiss with the guy didn't mean anything. She knew from experience that not all men equated love with fidelity. Some could profess love to one woman but have no problem screwing around with another.

On the other hand, two years had passed since Garrett had been in Colombia. Quite possibly, he and the missionary were no longer together. Whatever. It didn't really matter. What did matter was whether her interpretation matched what Garrett had experienced. She just hoped he didn't view the botched love scene as a mockery of what he and Helena had shared.

As she saw Garrett's features tighten, she nearly groaned in despair. What had she been thinking to believe she could even try to replicate what he'd shared with the Dutch missionary? She was an idiot.

"You know what?" She raised her hands. "Just forget I asked. It was a stupid request, and I'm sorry I bothered you with it. I'll leave." She turned away, intent only on getting out of there with what remained of her dignity. She had her hand on the screen door when Garrett's deep voice stopped her in her tracks.

"I'll do it."

Slowly, Ivy faced him. He stood, unmoving, in the center of the room, regarding her through hooded eyes. In the indistinct light, she couldn't read his expression, but she sensed the tension coiled within him.

He dominated the small room. Even dressed in jeans and a T-shirt, with his feet bare, he exuded raw energy. His dark hair fell forward around his face, shadowing his features and making his expression unreadable. He might be standing loose limbed and relaxed, but Ivy wasn't fooled. Energy rolled off the guy in waves, and the only thing she could think was that he was…dangerous.

Not for the first time, she wondered about the wisdom of her great idea. After all, what did she really know about Garrett Stokes? Nothing except what she'd read in the script.

He'd spent several years as a covert-ops specialist, crawling through the jungles of Colombia, destroying coca fields and labs and gathering intelligence about the most ruthless of the drug cartels. He'd killed men. He'd been tortured beyond what most people could endure and had survived. Even injured, he'd managed to escape his captors and evade those who pursued him for two days.

The guy was his own commando unit, and she'd just

asked him to give her *pointers* on making love. She was completely lame. She was probably the only woman on the face of the planet who couldn't get aroused by Eric Terrell's kisses, and she'd just asked a hardened soldier to give her *pointers*. She'd be lucky if she didn't find herself raped.

But in the next instant, she knew she was wrong. She was safe with Garrett; at least, she amended silently, as safe as she wanted to be. If she was honest with herself, she wanted him. She'd wanted him even *before* he'd kissed her, but since that night she'd thought of little else except what it would be like to make love with Garrett Stokes.

She'd come out to the *casita* on the pretext of learning more about Helena's character, but a little voice inside her said that was all an act. She'd come out tonight because she wanted to find out what it was like to be with Garrett. He was unlike any man she'd ever known, but more than that, she felt a connection with him, a recognition of sorts.

"Are you sure?" she finally managed to say. "Because if you're not, I don't want to, you know…*force* you or anything. I mean, I only want you to do this if you're completely comfortable with the idea." God, she was babbling like an idiot but couldn't stop. "If you're not—"

"I said I'd do it."

His voice was rough, and when Ivy looked into his eyes, they seemed to shimmer, as though someone had lit a flame behind those flecked amber irises. As she took in the banked heat in his eyes, a disturbing awareness curled in her stomach.

"Right. I mean, that's great." Ivy drew a deep breath

and willed her rioting pulse to slow down. "I really appreciate your willingness to do this for me."

Yeah, right. Once again she knew she was not being honest with herself, that she wasn't doing this to gain a better understanding of Helena or his relationship with her, but was doing this for herself. Because she found Garrett intensely attractive, and just had to know what it would be like to be with him. She couldn't cease thinking about him, about his face and his expressions, his hands, his easy smile. No, it had nothing to do with Helena, and everything to do with her.

He smiled then, a lazy tilting of his lips that caused something hot and sensual to unfurl deep within her.

"Ma'am," he began, his voice no more than a rasp, "the pleasure is all mine. So...where do you want to start?"

At my mouth, and you can work your way down from there.

For a shocked instant, Ivy thought she'd actually uttered the words. But, no, his expression hadn't changed. His gaze, however, fastened on her mouth as if perhaps he'd read her thoughts and was giving them serious consideration.

Disconcerted by his stare, she nervously moistened her lips. "Ah, maybe you could tell me about Helena," she suggested breathlessly.

"What do you want to know?"

Could she be that truthful with him? "Well, maybe you could tell me what it was that attracted you to each other," Ivy said. "That, and what happened between the two of you during the days you hid beneath the mission church."

The smile he gave her was one of pure, male satisfaction. "A better question would be, what *didn't* happen?"

Immediately, images swamped Ivy's mind. Images

of him and a woman entwined on a narrow bed. And not just any woman.

Her.

She cleared her throat as warmth flooded her veins and a peculiar heaviness settled in her breasts. "So the attraction between the two of you was...instantaneous?"

For just a moment, something flickered in his eyes. Something hot and needful that caused her chest to tighten and her breath to hitch. In the next moment, the look was gone, and Ivy wondered if she'd imagined it.

He nodded. "Uh, yeah, pretty much." He cleared his throat, as if he wasn't entirely comfortable with the subject, but he didn't look away. If anything, the expression in his eyes appeared almost challenging, as if he half expected her to scoff at him. "It happened just like it says in the script."

"So there you were, injured and unconscious, and she had no choice but to remove your clothes and tend your wounds, even tearing strips from her own clothing to use as makeshift bandages." Ivy arched a eyebrow. "They didn't have a first-aid station at the mission?"

"Yeah, well, the place was swarming with cartel, and she didn't want to risk being caught carrying bandages and medical supplies into the church." He turned away to pull two bottles of beer out of the small fridge in the makeshift kitchen. He slid her a sideways glance. "I was delirious, and she spent hours sponging my brow and body with cool water. She never left my side. When I finally regained consciousness, there she was...my guardian angel."

His voice was impersonal, as if he disliked talking about those days. He turned back toward her as he pried the cap from the beer in his hand and extended the bottle to her. "And that was it. The rest, as they say, is history."

The tightness in Ivy's chest intensified, making it difficult for her to catch her breath, and a moment passed before she recognized the tightness for what it was—longing. That longing to experience firsthand what it would be like to be on the receiving end of Garrett's attentions. Even now, when he was being politely deferential and keeping his distance, he was compelling. She could only imagine how completely irresistible he would be when he set his mind on seduction.

She accepted the beer from his outstretched hand. "So far, you haven't told me anything I don't already know. I mean, all that is in the script."

She sounded peevish, but she couldn't help it. She was unprepared when he set his own beer down on the stone counter and closed the short distance between them, invading her space until she instinctively stepped backward. Her rear encountered the edge of the rough-hewn table, but still he came, crowding her.

She gasped when his big hands encircled her waist and lifted her onto the table, and he stood between her knees. The movement pushed the skirt of her dress high up on her legs. The sight of her bare thighs bracketing his denim-clad hips momentarily transfixed her.

"So what is it, *exactly,* that you want to know?" he demanded softly. He cupped her jaw in one warm, callused hand and tilted her face back, searching her eyes. "What it was like when I kissed her here?" He traced the pad of his thumb over her lower lip, his gaze never leaving hers. "Or here?" He stroked the back of his fingers along her jaw and down the side of her neck, causing shivers up and down her spine. She stopped breathing when his fingertips trailed over her collarbone and came to rest on the smooth skin below, exposed by the open collar of her dress. "Or how about…here?"

Ivy dragged in a shuddering breath as her body reacted to his touch. He was so near she could see the stubble that shadowed his lean jaw. She breathed in his male scent. Everything about him was pure, unadulterated male. The rough fabric of his jeans brushed against the sensitive skin of her inner thighs, and she had an overwhelming urge to wrap her legs around him and draw him nearer still.

The cold beer fell from her nerveless fingers, but she scarcely noticed as the bottle rolled off the table and clattered onto the floor in a froth of fragrant foam.

"What is it you want to know, Ivy?" His voice was low and insistent, his lips a mere breath from her own. He splayed his fingers across her upper chest until she was certain he could feel the frantic beating of her heart. "Tell me."

"Everything," she whispered raggedly, and watched, mesmerized, as he lowered his head toward her.

6

GARRETT COULD SCARCELY believe it. After two years of fantasizing about this woman, here he was *kissing* her, and this time there was no chance they'd be interrupted. Any second, he'd wake up and realize it was just another freaking dream, and he'd find himself alone and frustrated.

But this was better than any dream he'd ever had.

Her lips were incredibly soft. She tasted like wild honey and sweet arousal. It was a total turn-on. Garrett wanted to devour her, to spread her across the table and take her in the most primal way there was.

Instead, he used his lips to test hers and coax a response. She stiffened at the first touch of his mouth against her own, and beneath his palm, her breathing stopped. Still, he continued, planting small kisses along the closed seam of her mouth. He used his teeth to nip at the fullness of her lower lip.

He knew the moment her resistance melted. She exhaled on a helpless sigh and her entire body sagged. Garrett made a sound of approval and slanted his lips across hers, licking and nibbling and taking complete advantage of her small sigh to gain access to her mouth and sweep his tongue inside.

She tasted dark and hot and potent. He cupped the lush curves of her buttocks and pulled her forward, to the very edge of the table. Through the thin material of her dress, her skin was warm against his palms.

She moaned softly, before winding her arms around his neck. One hand tangled itself in his hair, while the other clutched his back and drew him nearer.

Garrett complied, drawing her into his arms until her breasts were crushed against his chest. He urged her hips closer, pushing himself against the juncture of her thighs until he could feel her, hot and needy, against the front of his button-fly jeans.

He couldn't remember the last time he'd been this hard for a woman. His blood roared in his ears, and his senses were filled with the taste and feel of her.

"Oh, God," she panted, dragging her lips away. "I don't—I didn't mean—" She broke off. Her breathing was ragged, her expression dazed.

"Hey," he murmured, cradling her face in his hands and smoothing a thumb over her lip. His own breathing was a little uneven. "It's okay. We're just moving too fast." He bent his head so he could look into her eyes. "I'll slow down. Okay?"

When she raised her eyes to him, Garrett's heart nearly stopped at the raw desire on her face. "Is that how it was with Helena?" Her voice was husky. "Slow? Did you go slowly with her?"

He tilted his head in bemusement. "What?"

For several endless seconds, he had absolutely no clue what she was talking about. Then he remembered. *Damn.* One kiss, and he'd forgotten all about Helena and the reason Ivy was even there in the first place. It wasn't because she was hot for *him;* it was because she needed pointers on how to make her on-screen love scenes rock.

"No," he growled. "We didn't take it slow." He didn't

want to talk about Helena, didn't want to tell Ivy that he and the missionary hadn't taken it slow, fast or otherwise. They hadn't taken it, period.

He tipped her face up, ignoring her gasp. She was so close that his breath disturbed the loose tendril of hair that had fallen against her temple. Her own breathing was shallow and rapid. Her fingers still curled around the back of his neck, and he was still pressed against the warm, sweet cradle of her hips. He felt her fingers tighten fractionally, and then she looked at him from beneath her lashes.

"Then I don't want to go slow, either."

The words emerged in a rush, and Garrett needed a few seconds to process what she'd said, and what it meant.

She didn't want to go slow.

"Sweetheart—"

"Shh." Whatever he'd been about to say, she halted him with her fingers against his lips. "Don't talk. Just show me—show me what it was like to be her…with you."

Her eyes searched his, and seeing the need in those shimmering espresso depths undid him. He groaned and slid his hands along her jaw, cradling her face in his palms and stroking the sensitive skin with the pads of his thumbs. But despite the fact that every male hormone in his body raged for him to take her, a part of him needed to make her understand his desire for her was real and had nothing to do with Helena Vanderveer. To tell Ivy fictitious stories about what had supposedly transpired between him and the missionary was one thing. To take advantage of Ivy like this was another thing altogether.

"Wait, Ivy," he rasped, covering her fingers with his and pulling them away from his lips. "There's something important I have to tell you—"

"I don't want to know." She squeezed her thighs around his and tunneled her hands into his hair, drawing his face down for another soul-wrenching kiss. "I just want to feel," she breathed against his lips. "I want to feel what Helena felt…see what she saw…know what she knew…"

As if to make her meaning clear, she gave him a deep, openmouthed kiss, while at the same time wrapping her legs around his hips and pressing against him in an unmistakable invitation.

It was his undoing.

All thoughts of spilling his guts vanished, along with any vestiges of self-control. He'd wanted this for too long. If Ivy knew the truth—that there had been no romance with Helena—she'd be gone quicker than he could say *hasta la vista, baby.*

With a groan of surrender, Garrett slid his hands beneath her buttocks and lifted her off the table. She made a soft sound of surprise, but didn't protest. She just deepened the kiss and hung on.

Gripping her luscious bottom, her bare thighs clenched around his waist, Garrett turned and, in three easy strides, crossed to the bed and shoved the mosquito netting aside, then lowered himself onto the pillows. The weight of Ivy's body on his was exquisite torture, but with her now straddling his hips, he had free access to her delectable backside.

He pushed his hands beneath the bunched-up skirt of her dress and stroked his palms along the outside of her thighs, reveling in the feel of her bare skin. She squirmed on top of him, rubbing herself against the hard ridge of his arousal. He wanted badly to touch her, to slide the insubstantial barrier of her panties aside and explore her thoroughly.

Instead, he reached up and pulled her ponytail free

of the elastic band that held it. Her hair tumbled forward around her face in a fragrant mass of springy curls. He thrust his fingers into the silken corkscrews and caught her lower lip between his teeth, alternately nipping and then soothing the tender flesh with his tongue.

She made a soft sound of pleasure, and then her hands fisted in the material of his T-shirt, pushing it up until she could slide her palms beneath the hem. His stomach muscles contracted beneath her fingers. She pushed higher, smoothing her hands over his skin and trailing her fingertips across his nipples, pausing there to explore the hard nubs. She dragged her lips from his and, as he sucked wind, skated her mouth along his jaw until she caught his earlobe between her teeth.

Heat jackknifed through him, spiraled through his midsection. When her hands slid lower and lingered over the button of his jeans, he stopped breathing. For the space of a heartbeat, neither of them moved.

Sensing her hesitation, Garrett reached down and captured her hand in his. "I want this, babe," he rasped, "but only if you're sure."

"I am." Her breath hitched. "Please…let me."

Garrett groaned again. He was riding a wave of pure, unadulterated lust, and nothing short of an act of God would prevent him from letting Ivy have her way.

"Ah, sweetheart," he said, his voice husky, "I'm all yours."

IVY KNEW SHE WAS GOING too far, but she was too far gone to care. Even the knowledge that she was just a substitute for the woman he really wanted wasn't enough to cool the molten heat of desire that flowed through her. His touch, combined with the hot, sexy expression in his eyes, was enough to make her lose her head. She could actually feel her brain cells blinking off one by one.

With one hand braced on his muscular chest, she used her other to unfasten the button on the front of his jeans. Her knuckles brushed against the hard thrust of his erection beneath the denim, and she didn't miss how he sucked in his breath at the contact. The knowledge that she could affect him—a tough, uncompromising soldier—with a mere touch was heady stuff. It was almost enough to make up for the fact she was no more than a stand-in for the woman he really wanted.

Ivy slowly unbuttoned his jeans and then, sweet heaven—the guy was going commando. Ivy didn't think she'd ever seen anything as gorgeous as his long, thick erection, dark against the paler skin of his abdomen. Desire, sharp and fierce, knifed through her. More than a year had passed since she'd been in any kind of relationship, and she'd almost forgotten what it was like to want a guy so badly she physically ached; to anticipate touching him, tasting him…taking him.

She swallowed hard and glanced up at Garrett's face. His features were drawn taut, and his eyes glowed in the indistinct light as he watched her. He used one hand to sweep her hair back from her face, and then bent his free arm behind his head. The gesture said clearly she could do as she pleased.

Emboldened by the heat in his eyes, Ivy slipped her fingers around his shaft, her heart thudding in her chest. He was large, no question about it; he was probably impressive even when not aroused. If this is what Helena Vanderveer had glimpsed when bathing Garrett's injured body, no wonder she'd wanted to nurse him back to health with her own hands. The guy gave a whole new meaning to the term *hardened soldier*.

"Oh, my," she murmured in appreciation, devouring him with her eyes. He has like hot silk beneath her hand. In awe, she smoothed a thumb across the blunted head of his erection. When it came away slick with moisture, an answering heat pooled in her center. Unable to resist, she circled her fingers around him.

He jerked reflexively in her hand and made a deep sound of pleasure. When she glanced at him, the expression in his eyes—hot and intense—consumed her, made her want to see just how far she could go before he completely lost control. It had nothing to do with re-creating a Helena scenario and everything to do with how he made her feel: sexy and desirable. With the heavy weight of him cradled in her hand, she suddenly needed to find out if he tasted as good as he looked.

"I don't know, soldier," she mused aloud, sending him what she hoped was a sultry look, "your situation appears...dire."

He smiled fractionally, but Ivy didn't miss how his muscles tightened as she squeezed him gently, before sliding her hand down the length of him, then back up again. "Yeah," he agreed, his voice husky. "I'm not sure how much longer I'll last. What do you recommend?"

"Well, first of all..." Ivy scooted back on his thighs a bit. "We'll need to do something to relieve the... pressure." She bent forward and, without giving him time to react, took him in her mouth.

He made a strangled sound of surprise and pleasure, and then shifted his hips, shoving his jeans down his thighs to give her better access. Ivy murmured her approval, and with one hand still wrapped around him, she swirled her tongue over him, thrilling to his taste and texture. The feel of him beneath her palm was an aphrodisiac. He was smooth and slick against her tongue, and she slid her mouth over him, taking as much of him as she could. She alternately suckled and licked him, reveling in the throaty noises he was making. She squeezed the base of his shaft and, with her free hand, cupped him from below, lightly raking her fingernails across his sac until it was drawn up tight beneath him.

The noises of intense pleasure he was making, combined with the tightening of his muscles, told her he was close to climaxing. She wasn't prepared when, with a groan, Garrett lifted her away from him and bore her backward until suddenly, she was pinned against the mattress by the weight of his body.

"My turn." The promise implicit in his voice sent erotic shivers of anticipation down Ivy's spine.

"But I didn't finish," she protested weakly.

"Sweetheart," he growled softly, "any more and you'll kill me." He dipped his head and pressed a kiss to the sensitive skin beneath her ear. "And you don't want to do that before I have a chance to give you a few pointers."

Pointers. There was that word again. Ivy realized it had the ability to arouse her as much as it was beginning to infuriate her. Had she really said she wanted *pointers?* Right now, all she wanted was him, hot and hard between her thighs.

Still, she couldn't stop the words that sprang to her lips. "Is this how it was with Helena?" she asked, breathlessly, as if she'd just sprinted a mile. Ivy knew she shouldn't care what he'd shared with Helena, or even if he still cared for the other woman. This was business. It was about rescuing her lackluster love scenes, and no matter how enjoyable she might find this, there was nothing *personal* about it.

Nothing.

Not even when he rocked slowly against her, letting her feel his hard heat against her core. Not even when he reached beneath her and cupped a buttock, then slid his hand underneath the elastic band of her panties to massage her bare skin.

"Stop thinking," he commanded thickly, as if reading her thoughts. His breathing was ragged against her neck. "Just feel."

Flames licked along the underside of her skin, and liquid desire pooled at her center. Desperate for the taste of him, she turned her face toward his and sought his lips with her own. But Garrett didn't just kiss her; he devoured her. He stole her breath with the fierceness of his kiss, sweeping his tongue inside her mouth. She met him eagerly, drawing him deeper as she threaded her fingers through the warm silk of his hair.

She was unprepared when he pushed aside the fragile barrier of her panties and stroked her intimately, parting her soft folds and swirling his finger over her slick flesh.

She dragged her mouth from his. *"Ohmigod."*

The sensation of his touching her was electric, and she pushed helplessly against his hand.

"You're so wet." His voice was low and rough. "So responsive."

"It's—it's been a long time," she gasped in explanation. That was why she was soaked with desire for him, why she was greedy for the feel of his flesh. It was no more than her body's long-suppressed needs finally demanding fulfillment.

His fingers worked magic between her legs. Fierce need sliced through her, and she knew it wouldn't take much to push her over the edge. Even now she could feel her orgasm building, her inner muscles tightening in anticipation. Garrett used the pad of his thumb to circle her clitoris, until she arched against him with a soft cry of distress.

"That's it, sweetheart." He claimed her mouth again, thrusting his tongue against hers even as he inserted a finger inside her. She came in a shattering explosion of sensation that left her shuddering and weak. He didn't release her, just continued stroking her until, unbelievably, she felt the beginnings of yet another orgasm. It blossomed within her, an insistent ache that made her long to wrap her legs around him and bring him completely inside her.

"Garrett," she whispered against his lips, "please…"

Was that *her* voice that sounded so needy? She couldn't believe she was begging this man—a stranger in nearly every respect—to have sex with her. She'd never done anything like this in her entire life, not even when she'd been in college. But there was no denying she wanted him, with an urgency she couldn't recall feeling for any other man, ever.

Garrett kissed her languorously, as if he had all the time in the world, as if he had no clue she was going out of her mind with wanting him. "Oh, man," he breathed, "somebody pinch me. I've dreamed of you for so long."

What? Ivy tilted her face back to look at him, smiling uncertainly. "You have?"

To her dismay, he jerked his head up and stared at her with something like horror in his eyes, as if he was seeing her for the first time. Before she could ask him what was wrong, he swore softly and snatched himself away from her body. Disentangling himself from her legs, he got up and yanked his pants up over his hips.

Bereft at his abrupt withdrawal, Ivy surreptitiously

adjusted her panties and smoothed her dress down over her thighs. Her body still thrummed with sensual vibrations, but all of a sudden she felt awkward and unwelcome. She pushed herself to a sitting position, watching him. He stood with one hand braced on the kitchen table, head bent. Every muscle in his body screamed with tension. Clearly, he was upset, but whether with himself or her she couldn't tell.

Recalling the shocked expression in his eyes as he'd looked at her, she suspected he'd gotten more than a little carried away in pretending she was Helena. He'd actually forgotten who he was with. For just that instant, he'd believed she *was* Helena.

"I'm sorry," he said over his shoulder. "I didn't mean that. I wasn't thinking clearly."

His words only confirmed what she already knew— physically he'd been with her, but the rest of him—the part that mattered—had been with someone else. A peculiar heaviness settled into her chest.

"That's okay." She stood up and fished around on the bed for her elastic before smoothing her hair back with both hands and capturing the thick mass into a ponytail. She stood for a moment, staring at his back. "This whole thing is my fault. I, um, pretty much took advantage of you." She chewed her lip. "Sorry."

He spun around then, his expression incredulous. "You think you took advantage of me?"

She spread her hands. "Well…yes. I came here and practically begged you to have sex with me." She drew in a deep breath and forced a smile. "At least we didn't let it go that far, right?"

One black eyebrow arched. His hair was disheveled where she'd thrust her fingers through it. His jeans were still unbuttoned, and through the open vee of denim, she caught a tantalizing glimpse of the lightly furred skin beneath. He looked incredibly sexy. But when he rubbed his jaw and partially turned away from her, she realized that apparently it didn't matter how she felt about their brief interlude. It obviously bothered him.

She infused a bright note into her voice, determined not to let him see her hurt. "You know what? I'm just going to leave now. We can pretend this never even happened."

She made a beeline for the screened door, startled when he stepped into her path and blocked her with his body.

"Ivy." His voice was low.

"No, don't say it," she implored. "It's fine, really." She searched his eyes. "I'm not a little girl, and I came here tonight with my eyes wide-open. I know that what you shared with Helena was special, and I don't want to take anything away from that. I realize I'm not her…"

God, she was making a mess of it. She closed her eyes and struggled to collect her thoughts. "I just wanted to feel a little of what she must have felt when she was with you. Because if I can't feel that, then I might as well pack my bags and go back to New York right now."

He muttered a curse and turned away from her, raking a hand through his hair. When he spun back around, his eyes glinted dangerously and his voice was rough. "What I shared with Helena—well, let's just say it wasn't about sex."

Ivy cringed at the derision in his voice. "I realize that. But it's the love scenes that reveal to the audience just how deeply you cared for each other. I was just hoping that—that I could…"

Her voice trailed away as she realized how shallow she sounded. But, really, what was she supposed to say? *I was just hoping I could use you for sex so that I could*

*figure out how to shoot the love scenes, and, oh, by the
way, you have a great ass, so it's no hardship for me to
sleep with you? Nice.*

"Listen. I'd be lying if I told you I don't want to…
You're a beautiful woman…but that doesn't…"

The guy was actually flustered. Which was so unexpected it gave Ivy a little courage. She knew he found
her attractive. Regardless of how he felt about Helena,
he'd definitely had a physical response to *her*, Ivy. And
nobody was going to tell her that in the few short days
he'd spent with Helena, their connection to each other
hadn't started with a good healthy dose of lust. Okay,
so maybe it had developed into something more after
they'd gotten to know each other, but initially at least,
it had to have been all about the physical relationship,
and *that* Ivy and Garrett could replicate.

"Three days," she said softly. "Just spend the next
three days with me, until Finn and the others return from
Xalapa. After that, you don't even need to acknowledge
me if you don't want to. I won't expect anything from
you afterward, if that's what you're worried about."

He stared at her in disbelief. "So, what—we spend
the next three days locked together in this cabin, trying
to re-create the time I spent with Helena so that you can
go back and re-create it with *Terrell?*"

For several endless seconds, there was nothing but
silence. "Let me get this straight," he continued, his
voice tight. "You want me to pretend you're Helena. You
actually don't care if I think about another woman when
I'm with you?"

If Ivy hadn't known better, she'd have thought he
was angry. She gestured helplessly. "Well, nobody says
you *have* to think about her. But if it helps you to, you
know, get in the mood…" Although, really, to Ivy's

way of thinking, it didn't take much to get Garrett in the mood. They hadn't even bothered to undress and he'd been totally turned on.

And he hadn't been the only one.

Ivy could hardly believe she'd almost had sex with Garrett Stokes. She'd known the guy for all of a week, had exchanged no more than a handful of words with him, and had been in his cabin for less than ten minutes before they'd fallen on each other like a couple of horny teenagers.

She was pretty sure that if she hadn't jolted him back to reality, they *would* have had sex. Part of her wanted to weep that she hadn't just kept her mouth shut, pretended she hadn't heard his ragged confession about Helena and let him continue working magic on her body. She'd been ready to combust, and that had just been from what he'd done to her with his hands. She almost couldn't wait to see what he could do with his mouth…and the rest of his body.

And what was it, exactly, about him that made her forget her good sense? Okay, so the guy had the most amazing eyes she'd ever seen, and a body that just didn't quit, but she'd worked with some pretty hot costars and none had tempted her as much as this man did. Even the few actors she *had* been involved with hadn't made her lose control the way Garrett had.

Her heart thudded so loudly in her ears she thought for sure he must hear it. She couldn't believe what she'd just suggested, and as much as she told herself that coming to the *casita* had been a career move, a part of her acknowledged anew there was another reason for her wanton request. She wanted him. Badly.

Even if it meant setting aside her own identity to have him.

"In other words," he said grimly, interrupting her thoughts, "you're looking for a stud."

"I'm not looking for a stud," she said quietly, stung by his choice of words. "I'm looking for a mentor."

"A sex coach." His tone was gently mocking.

Ivy tipped her chin up. "I want to experience first-hand what Helena shared with you. After all, you were the one who said you'd be available to give me pointers if I needed them. You were the one who said I'd need to act out the love scenes as if I were with *you*." She took a step toward him. "So what's wrong? There's obviously no shortage of chemistry between us. Most guys would jump at the chance for three days of no-strings sex."

"Three days, huh?"

He was actually considering it. She should have been thrilled. Instead, she was mildly annoyed that he even had to think about it.

"Going once…going twice…"

He smiled then, and Ivy felt her stomach do a slow roll. He took a step toward her, and he was so close she could feel the heat radiating from his body. They stood like that for a full minute, and the heat in his eyes caused her heart rate to accelerate in anticipation.

"Fine," he finally said. "I'll do it…"

"Great—"

"On one condition."

"What's that?" Her voice was wary.

His smile turned predatory. "We play by my rules."

Ivy's pulse kicked into overdrive. "What do you mean?"

"I mean that I get to call the shots. I'm the one who has the firsthand experience of how this whole thing…went down…so I get to say how we re-create it."

Ivy's imagination surged, and she was helpless to control the tremor of excitement in her voice. "Okay, fair enough. When do we start?"

"We already have."

7

GARRETT LEANED BACK AGAINST the gnarled trunk of a Mayan breadnut tree and waited. From where he stood, about twenty feet behind the old workers' quarters, he had a clear view of his *casita* and the path that led to the hacienda. Unable to sleep, he'd been out there for a couple of hours. His *casita* had suddenly seemed too small, too closed in for him. Ivy's fragrance still lingered there, and he couldn't so much as look at his bed without remembering her on it.

He was soaked through to his skin from the brief, tropical downpour that had moved through the region during the dark, predawn hours. The surrounding foliage was heavy with moisture, and the ground beneath his feet was soggy. Around him, the forest was unrelentingly black and silent but for the continuous drip of water from the lush canopy.

Raising his arm, he peered at the illuminated face of his watch. It was just past 5:00 a.m. If Ivy was lucky, she'd managed to grab at least a few hours of the sleep that had eluded him.

Nope, sleeping definitely hadn't been an option for him, not when the evening's amazing events had replayed themselves over and over again in his head. Ivy in his cottage, with her gorgeous lips wrapped around him…Ivy writhing beneath him, her face an exquisite masterpiece of erotic pleasure. Both were images he'd never forget. Christ, he grew hard just remembering what they'd done together.

He'd been so caught up in the moment he'd completely forgotten that he was supposed to be playing a part. He recalled again the dumb-ass thing he'd said during the red-hot heat of the moment.

I've dreamed of you for so long.

He still couldn't believe he'd uttered the words. For one, brief second, he'd thought Ivy realized it was *her* he'd been talking about, and it had scared the hell out of him. How did you tell a woman you were about to nail—under a totally false pretext—that you'd secretly followed her career for two years and harbored an intense crush on her, without her thinking you were some kind of creepy stalker?

You didn't.

He'd royally screwed up when he'd let those words slip out, but it wouldn't happen again. If anything, his mistake reinforced his belief that he was growing soft, that he'd been away from Spec-Ops for too long. He should have better control over his thoughts and emotions. A slip like that one could have cost him his life back when he was an operator.

And that hadn't been the only snafu of the night. He'd told her that he'd be the one to call the shots on how the love scenes would be re-created, but immediately after walking her back to the hacienda, he'd wondered just what the hell he'd gotten himself into. He had no freaking clue how to re-create the love scenes Ivy wanted, given that *there had been no love scenes with Helena Vanderveer.*

He'd struggled briefly with his conscience over that one, knowing he was taking unfair advantage of the situation. If Ivy discovered the deception, she might never forgive him. Even if he wanted to tell her the truth, he risked her finding out that the only reason she'd been cast as Helena in the first place was that he had some major pull with the director. That would go over real well.

Yep, it just kept getting better and better.

So he'd been awake all night, debating the pros and pitfalls of the plan he'd set into action. He had come close to convincing himself he was the biggest scumbag on the face of the planet for even thinking about going through with it.

Then he'd recall the scent of her skin, the texture of her lips beneath his; remember the hitch in her breathing as he'd pulled her close, and known there had never been any question whether he'd do it. Whatever else he might be, he was also a healthy, red-blooded male, and Ivy James roused every masculine instinct in him. *There was no way he wouldn't go through with it.* Being with Ivy was a physical imperative he couldn't ignore.

Despite his familiarity with the script, he'd read through it again swiftly, his mind furiously working out a strategy on how to bring it to life. He'd tried to imagine what it would be like to actually find himself in the situation called out in the script—not just the part where he was rescued, but where he found himself irresistibly drawn to his rescuer. It wasn't all that difficult. All he'd had to do was substitute Helena's face with Ivy's. The joy of being one with her would be heightened by the knowledge that it might be their only time together.

Garrett gave a self-deprecating laugh. The scenario was more true to life than he cared to admit. In the end, he'd decided to go with the screenplay as written. But he'd drawn the line at having Ivy find him, bloodied, filthy and unconscious in the dense forest behind the mission. So he'd made some minor modifications.

He glanced at his watch again. Exactly twelve minutes had passed since he'd sent Carlos, the cook's younger son, to bang on Ivy's door and wake her up with a fictitious story of an accident. The kid's English wasn't all that bad and he hadn't needed long to memorize the lines Garrett wanted him to recite. Garrett was willing to bet that with the added incentive of 250 pesos in his pocket, Carlos would do a great job with his first acting gig.

As if on cue, Garrett saw her. Ivy made her way swiftly along the dark path toward his *casita,* and Garrett's heart just about stopped when he saw she wore only a white bathrobe belted around her waist, and the same pair of slip-on sandals she'd had on the day she'd arrived in Pancho Viejo. If she wore anything at all under the robe, it had to be minuscule. Every stride she took caused the front of the robe to billow open, exposing her long, slender, bare legs. Beneath the thin material of the robe, her breasts bounced enticingly.

Her hair was loose around her shoulders, and even in the predawn darkness, Garrett could see her tense expression. She was worried about *him.* Determinedly, he pushed down the guilt that surged through him. They'd made an agreement. He needed to keep reminding himself of that. He wasn't acting in a vacuum here.

The thought almost made him laugh. The kicker was, he wasn't even acting. He'd never had as visceral a response to any woman as he'd had to Ivy.

He blew his breath out forcefully as he watched her. She reached the door of his *casita* and knocked imperiously.

"Garrett?" Her voice sounded strained. "Are you all right? Carlos got me. He said you weren't well…that there'd been an accident." When there was no response, she put her hand on the latch. "Garrett, I'm coming in."

IVY STEPPED INTO THE CABIN. A small kerosene lantern had been lit and placed on a low stool near the door, but it did little to penetrate the cabin's dark corners. She stood for a moment in the center of the room, letting her eyes adapt to the gloom. She wouldn't even try to adjust the brightness of the lantern. She'd never been an out-doorsy kind of girl, and as far as she was concerned, messing around with kerosene lanterns definitely fell into the category of outdoor activities.

"Garrett?" In the absolute stillness, her voice sounded abnormally loud and she immediately felt foolish, since it was apparent she was alone.

What the hell was going on? She'd been wide-awake, tossing and turning against her pillows when the boy, Carlos, had rapped on her door and let loose a stream of frantic Spanish, none of which she'd understood. Until he'd uttered Garrett's name in the same breath as the word *accident*. The frantic look on his face, combined with the urgency of his tone, had galvanized her into action. She'd wanted to awaken somebody— one of the other cast members, at the very least—but the boy had made it clear she was to *hurry*.

Now she wondered if she wasn't the target of a joke. She could make out the silhouette of the bed and the ghostly drape of mosquito netting that enveloped it. The bedding was no more than a dark heap beneath the netting, but no way was she going to explore the shadowy recesses.

Feeling foolish that she'd been duped, she turned

abruptly to leave—and gasped as she bumped up against something hard and damp.

"I'm touched that you didn't even stop to change before you raced here to rescue me," drawled a deep, unmistakable voice.

"Garrett." His presence shocked her. She was certain the cabin had been empty when she'd arrived, yet she hadn't heard him enter behind her. She'd had no idea he was even there until she'd encountered his solid warmth. Realizing her hands were curled in the damp fabric of his shirt, she released him and quickly stepped back. "You're soaked. What happened to you?"

She sensed rather than saw him move forward, and she took an involuntary step back. But he kept on coming. She kept retreating, until she bumped against the edge of the table, which immediately brought to mind the last time she'd been in a similar situation. And look how *that* had ended.

"I'm injured." His voice was low and compelling. He walked forward until he was pressed against her from chest to knee. He radiated heat, and the moisture from his clothing seeped through the thin satin of her robe until even her skin was damp. His eyes glowed in the indistinct light. "My being here may put you in danger, but I had nowhere else to turn, do you understand?"

Ivy swept her gaze over his body. "You're injured? Where?" Her hands sought him again, searching for evidence of injury. "How? Carlos didn't say, or if he did, I couldn't understand."

Beneath her fingers, the muscles of his shoulders and arms tightened. But when she skimmed her hands over his chest and downward, he covered them with his own, halting further exploration.

"Trust me," he said drily. "I'm injured, and the

Escudero cartel is hunting me. If I don't find a safe place to hide out for a few days and recover, they *will* find me and kill me." His voice dropped meaningfully. "Will you let me hide here at the mission until I can rendezvous with my men?"

Suddenly, Ivy comprehended. She'd asked him when they would start their three-day reenactment, and he'd told her they already had. Adrenaline, hot and pulsing, surged through her as she realized why she was here. She struggled to conceal a smile. Garrett wasn't truly injured; he was acting, and not doing an especially great job of it, either.

After he'd walked her to the hacienda, she'd lain in bed and wondered just what it was she'd gotten herself into. Yes, she was an actress, but knowing that he wasn't an actor and that there was no film crew watching them changed everything. No matter how she tried to rationalize her actions, in the end it was just the two of them.

Having sex.

But Ivy wanted more. If she wanted to understand the depth of what he'd shared with Helena, she needed to bring an emotional element into their lovemaking. She needed to believe she was in love with Garrett, and that their time together might be limited to this brief interlude; that they might not survive long enough or have a second chance to fully explore their feelings. Every gesture, every caress, every whispered endearment had to convey how she felt. She needed to become Helena.

Recalling the intensity of his eyes when he watched her, she'd thought she'd be much too self-conscious to actually go through with her proposed plan. But now, with him standing before her, heat washed over her and she was mildly shocked at just how much she wanted to do this.

She *would* do this. She'd practically begged him to do this; she told herself once more that being with Garrett was necessary in order for her to portray the character of Helena as accurately as possible. All she had to do was check her inhibitions and her identity at the door.

She drew in a deep breath, aware this might possibly be the most demanding performance she'd ever give, both physically and emotionally.

"I can hide you here," she said breathlessly, entwining her fingers through his. "The cartel sometimes raids the mission, but they don't know about this room. How badly are you injured?"

"My leg is pretty busted up."

"Let's get you over to the bed." Ivy slid an arm under his, wrapping it around his slim waist. He leaned heavily on her, and it was all Ivy could do not to stagger beneath him. She used both hands to support him as they made their way slowly around the table, toward the bed, heat still rolling off his body despite his clothing. Pushing the mosquito netting aside, he lowered himself across the mattress with a heartfelt groan.

"Okay," Ivy said, adopting a businesslike demeanor. Per the script, this was how Helena had acted after Garrett had been brought to the secret room. But for Ivy, it was also the only way she was going to get through the next scene. "Let's pull those jeans off and see what we're dealing with."

Avoiding his eyes, she bent over him, quickly undid the laces on his boots and slid his boots off, then pulled his socks off. Jeez, even his feet were big. She glanced uncertainly along the length of his body. He'd flung one arm across his eyes, shielding his expression from her view. She'd love to know what was going through his mind at this moment. Did he feel completely foolish trying to reenact the scene? Or, like her, was his heart rate accelerating with anticipation?

"Garrett, I need to get you out of these pants," she reiterated. Her hands hovered uncertainly over his belt buckle. "Can you help me?"

He raised his arm and gave her a lazy grin. "I thought you'd never ask."

"Ha-ha." Feeling slightly better, she worked the buckle on his belt and then undid the button on his jeans. "Lift your butt," she commanded. "I'm going to slide these off."

He did as ordered, and pushed his jeans down to his thighs.

Ivy looked, caught her breath and looked swiftly away. She'd already seen him, but the sight of his body robbed her of breath. He'd changed his clothes sometime after she'd left and, to her intense disappointment, was no longer going commando. He wore a pair of black briefs that hugged his flat stomach and slim hips. Ivy crouched by his feet. Deliberately keeping her eyes averted, she drew the pants carefully down his long legs and furtively admired the hard-hewn muscles that corded his thighs. She swallowed hard.

"So what, exactly, is the nature of your injury?" she asked, briefly stepping out of character and striving for a normal tone as she tugged the jeans free and folded them neatly on the floor beside his boots. "I mean, you're not going to make me go through the pretense of cleaning and stitching a wound that isn't really there, are you?"

But when she turned her attention back at his leg, the nature of his injury was clear, even after years of healing. Ivy felt the color drain from her face. Garrett's knee was a mass of raised scars that extended upward into his thigh and downward into the bunched muscle of his calf. Some of the scars were misshapen, ugly splotches; others were obviously the result of a surgeon's scalpel. Unable to help herself, she traced a finger over a wide, flat disk of scar tissue just above his knee that looked suspiciously like a healed bullet wound.

"What did they do to you?" she breathed.

"They shot me," he said drily. "The bullet went right through. Helena cleaned it and closed the entry and exit wounds. If you'd like, I can show you the matching scar on the back of my thigh."

He made a motion as if to raise his leg for her to view that scar. Ivy snapped her head up, and man, oh, man, he was right there. She swallowed. Over the intimate bulge of his briefs, the flat plane of his stomach and the hard thrust of his pecs beneath his T-shirt, she met his gaze. His eyes were all innocence, but she swore she detected a hint of dimple in one lean cheek.

"Um, I don't think that will be necessary," she said hastily, standing. He lay sprawled against the bedding, arms bent behind his head. The light from the nearby lantern cast intriguing shadows over the contours of his face, and his eyes held a dangerous glint as he watched her. He looked every inch like some flesh-and-bone fantasy there for her personal pleasure. Only with difficulty did she remember they had a script to follow.

"Your shirt is still wet," she commented, eyeing the fabric that clung damply to his chiseled chest. "You should probably take it off."

But when he sat up and dragged the T-shirt over his head then dropped it onto the floor, she nearly had to sit down herself. Garrett Stokes was hard *everywhere*. From his broad shoulders, down over his chest, to the

BUSINESS REPLY MAIL

FIRST-CLASS MAIL   PERMIT NO. 717   BUFFALO, NY

POSTAGE WILL BE PAID BY ADDRESSEE

Harlequin Reader Service

3010 WALDEN AVENUE

PO BOX 1867

BUFFALO NY 14240-9952

NO POSTAGE
NECESSARY
IF MAILED
IN THE
UNITED STATES

six-pack that rode above the waistband of his briefs, he was heart-stoppingly, supremely male.

He sported several nasty scars that traveled horizontally across his chest, as if somebody had slashed him repeatedly with a sharp blade. There was another long gash along his ribs. Unlike the scar on his knee, these scars had faded to pale silver. Ivy didn't want to think about how'd he'd gotten them.

He flung himself back onto the mattress and watched her through eyes heavy-lidded with desire. Against the abundance of bedding and pillows, he looked positively hedonistic. Her eyes traveled over the expanse of his chest and shoulders, and she had an overwhelming urge to run her hands over all that smooth, bronzed skin.

"So what now?" Even to her own ears, her voice sounded high and uncertain. Clearing her throat, she attempted for a more authoritative tone. "According to the script, you were unconscious for most of that first day."

Even in the indistinct light, there was no mistaking the lazy smile that curved his lips. "Why don't we jump ahead a page or two, to where Helena realizes the cartel is surveilling the mission and she has to spend the night in the secret room with her patient."

Ivy tried unsuccessfully to quell the tremor of anticipation that fluttered low in her abdomen. "By then, her patient has regained consciousness and she realizes there are other reasons she wants to stay, reasons that have nothing to do with avoiding the cartel, right?"

Garrett's eyes glowed. "Why don't we take it from the point where Helena undresses."

Ivy knew exactly which scene Garrett referred to; it was the same scene where she'd felt him observing her from the side of the set that first day of shooting. She'd wondered then what he thought of her. Now, as her hands drifted to the sash of her robe, she realized she wouldn't have to wonder any longer.

8

Her robe was made out of some shiny, silky material that slid along the contours of her body like liquid, revealing rather than concealing the outline of upturned breast, the inward dip of waist, the curve of hip and thigh. Even the dim lantern in the corner heightened the allure, casting her features in shadow and lending her an aura of exotic mystery.

Garrett was completely enthralled.

He'd decided when he'd walked through the door of the *casita* that he was into this all the way. There would be no self-recriminations, and no turning back. He'd even gone so far as to clear Ivy's schedule with the language coach and costume department for the next several days, ensuring none of the crew or other cast members would come looking for her.

Josephina, the hacienda's cook and Carlos's mother, had agreed to bring meals to the *casita* once each day. She hadn't so much as batted an eyelash at the request. Garrett suspected she was so happy not to be sharing her kitchen with Eric Terrell's personal chef, even for a few days, that she would have agreed to anything.

Ivy had asked for three days; he'd make sure she'd have his undivided attention every minute for the next seventy-two hours. At that moment, as Ivy's fingers dropped to the sash of her robe, nothing short of a full-scale artillery attack could have diverted his attention from her.

A part of him couldn't quite believe this was really happening. Here he was, alone with Ivy James in a hut in the Mexican mountains, and she was getting ready to remove her clothing for him. For *him*. It was a moment he'd never forget.

She glanced at him and caught her lower lip between her teeth in an unconscious gesture that spoke volumes; she wasn't nearly as confident as she'd have him believe.

"Go on," he encouraged gently. "Remember what Finn said. You're hugely attracted to me. You *want* me."

He saw her lips curve in a quick smile at the mild teasing in his tone, but he didn't miss how heat flared in her eyes. She *did* want him. The knowledge was like having gasoline tossed onto the banked flames of his desire.

He watched, mesmerized, as she unfastened the robe and let it fall open, and holy mother of God, she was wearing only a pair of panties and a little camisole that did nothing to hide her body from his greedy gaze. Her skin glowed softly in the dim light, and through the silky fabric of her top, her nipples were erect. He ached to touch them.

When he gazed into her face, he could tell she was self-conscious, and he tried to let her see how utterly gorgeous and desirable he found her.

"You're absolutely beautiful," he said, his voice husky.

Emboldened, she shrugged and the robe drifted to the floor in a whisper, to pool around her feet.

Garrett nearly stopped breathing. He'd seen her disrobe on the set, but only now, when she was turned fully toward him, could he truly appreciate the vision she made. She was the embodiment of everything he found feminine. Her skin was luminous, her body slim and supple. Her legs were long and slender, while her hips curved gently into a narrow waist.

She looked at him now and smiled. It was a smile that held both promise and expectation, and Garrett felt his body grow taut in response. He reminded himself that this might be the only time he'd have her like this, and something in his chest tightened. He would make this good for her; make it an experience she'd never forget.

"I want you here," he rasped, and patted the mattress beside him.

She didn't hesitate, but came over to him on all fours, like a sleek cat, her hair tumbling forward around her face in a dark cloud. "Are you sure?" Her voice was low and sexy. "After all, you're still recovering. I wouldn't want you to relapse."

"Sweetheart," he groaned, sliding his hands up the length of her arms, "if you don't touch me, I think I might die."

She laughed, a huff of breath that whispered across his skin and caused goose bumps to rise on his sensitized flesh. She was straddling him, her hands braced on either side of his head, and her lush breasts were right there, practically in his face.

"We wouldn't want that to happen," she said breathlessly. "Not after all the trouble I've been through to save you."

Sweetheart, he thought, *you've no idea.*

Without responding, he buried his hands in the fragrant mass of her hair and drew her down, covering her mouth in a heated kiss. She moaned and leaned against him, until he could feel her luscious breasts pressed against his chest. Heat lanced through him, and he deepened the kiss, sweeping his tongue inside her mouth. This time, she didn't need any encouragement, and she met him with a sweet fierceness that took his breath away, first tangling her tongue with his and then sucking on it, drawing it deeper. Her mouth was hot and potent.

As he angled her face for better access, she lowered her body and then, sweet Mary, he could feel her, rubbing back and forth over his throbbing erection. The sensation was so exquisite, so pleasurable, he wasn't certain he could stand it. While he wasn't exactly a monk, he hadn't been with anyone in a long time. His self-control was tenuous at best.

Without giving her a chance to protest, he turned her beneath him in one swift, smooth movement. She let out a small cry of surprise against his mouth, but then settled back against the pillows with a sigh of pleasure and wound her arms around his neck, feasting on his mouth.

Oh, yeah, this was perfect, except that now she was arching against him, rotating her hips against his in an invitation that was unmistakable.

Garrett dragged his mouth free and bent his forehead to hers, sucking in deep breaths. "Easy, sweetheart," he said in a strangled voice. "I don't want to go too fast, but if you keep that up, I'm not going to last."

Pleased, she gave a gurgle of laughter. "Really? But I thought you special-ops guys were all about patience and control."

Garrett raised his head and looked down into her flushed face. Her eyes were like warm chocolate and shimmered with arousal and need. Her mouth was swollen from his kisses, reminding him of a ripe strawberry. He wanted to bite her.

"Babe," he said, deliberately rotating his pelvis against hers so that she gasped and her eyes went hazy, "you've got it wrong. We're all about performing under pressure."

Propping himself on one elbow, he slid the strap of her camisole down over one shoulder, until the soft swell of a breast was revealed. He traced his fingertips over the creamy flesh, noting how her nipple tightened beneath the satin fabric. "As a senior operator, I play a vital role in elevating the…proficiency…of newly assigned personnel."

Ivy gave a tiny gasp as he drew the camisole down farther, and the rosy tip of her breast sprang free. "I see," she managed to say. She was breathless. "What else do you do?"

Garrett paused to devour the sight and then dipped his head to brush his lips over the hardened nub, before flicking it with his tongue. "On a daily basis, I prove myself to be highly skilled in all aspects of…sensitive…operations." He drew her nipple into his mouth, suckling it gently. He heard Ivy moan again, and laved the distended tip with his tongue. "I'm always ready to deploy—" he pressed his length against her core in a meaningful way "—either independently or as a team member, at a moment's notice." He filled his palm with her breast and gently rolled her nipple between his teeth, gratified when she bit her lip and shifted restlessly beneath him. "Beyond that, I constantly strive to improve my…skills…during off-duty time."

"Please…please." Her voice was ragged, and she cupped his face, dragging it upward so she could fasten her mouth against his and draw his very soul from between his lips.

That broken plea, combined with her molten kiss, was enough to push the last of his restraint over the edge. He'd intended to go slowly, to let her set the pace, but he hadn't counted on the intensity of his need for her. Heat spiraled downward through his midsection, and he felt his control stretch thin.

"You drive me crazy, you know," he muttered against her lips. "From the moment I first saw you, I wanted to know how you would feel in my hands. How you would taste…"

He slanted his mouth across hers, deepening the kiss, wanting to consume her, to eat her alive. She made a whimpering sound of need and arched against him, gliding her hands up over his shoulders to pull him closer. "I've wanted this, too," she whispered raggedly. "It's all I've thought about…you, in my arms."

Her words were intoxicating. He needed to be closer, with nothing separating them. He wanted to feel her skin against his, to absorb her heat. He pushed her camisole higher, wanting it gone completely, needing to see her. She helped him by pulling it over her head, and then she was completely naked but for the minuscule scrap of white silk at her crotch.

He almost stopped breathing.

Then he filled his hands with her breasts, admiring how full and firm they were, and how her nipples ripened beneath his fingers.

"Oh, God," she panted, shifting restlessly against him. "You have to touch me or I swear, I'm just going to die."

"But I *am* touching you," he rasped, smiling against her neck.

"No, I mean—you have to touch me…*there*."

Her plea was desperate, and lust jackknifed through Garrett. With a groan, he claimed her mouth, while at the same time he smoothed his hand down over the silken skin of her abdomen until he encountered the edge of her panties. With any other woman, he'd have slowed down. He'd have taken his time reaching this point, stretched the anticipation out over days, maybe even weeks. But he knew time was something they didn't have. Per the script—and in reality—this might be their only time together, and he wanted to experience all of her. Still, he hesitated.

Ivy made an incoherent sound of need and covered his hand with her own, pushing it downward. Requiring no further invitation, Garrett cupped her through the thin layer of silk. She was hot, and the fabric was wet with her desire. He could feel the soft contours of her folds through the insubstantial barrier, but it wasn't enough.

Pulling away from her, he reared up on his knees and positioned himself between her legs. Ivy watched him through glittering, half-closed eyes as he drew her panties down over her hips. She helped him by raising her legs and kicking the filmy material free, and then, there she was, completely exposed to his gaze.

Garrett thought he'd never seen anything as erotic or beautiful as Ivy James, spread naked across his bed with her knees bent. She stole his breath. Her feminine folds enticed him from beneath a narrow strip of dark curls.

"Oh, man," he groaned, "you are so incredibly, amazingly perfect." More perfect than even his CinemaScope fantasies had imagined. Ivy James on the big screen couldn't hold a candle to Ivy James in the flesh. He cupped her with one hand. Her skin was like the softest silk. When he parted her and slid a finger along her slick cleft, she cried out and arched against his hand.

"I need you…" she panted "…inside me."

Garrett grew even harder at her words. "Soon, baby," he promised. "There's just something I have to do first."

He pushed himself backward, then knelt on the floor by the edge of the bed and edged his hands beneath her buttocks. He devoured the sight of her, pink and plump and glistening with need, before trailing moist kisses along her inner thigh. She trembled beneath his touch. When he reached her core, he breathed in her scent, then pressed a kiss directly to her center. She bucked and cried out, clutching his head.

"I love the way you taste," he ground out, skating his lips along her inner thigh. "I love how good you smell."

Garrett was in heaven. Sweet, delicious heaven. He positioned her legs so they draped over his shoulders as he laved her with his tongue, while she made soft noises of intense pleasure and speared her fingers through his hair. Her breath came faster and the sounds she was making turned frantic. When he concentrated his efforts on the tiny bud of her clitoris and pushed his fingers into her, she bowed off the mattress and her whole body tautened until, with a cry of satisfaction, she convulsed beneath him.

IVY COULDN'T THINK. She could only lie sprawled across the bed, a helpless victim of the delicious aftershocks of what was possibly the most intense orgasm she'd ever experienced. Okay, definitely the most intense. Her entire body thrummed with sexual gratification. She was trembling. Sated and boneless, she was unprepared when Garrett slid his arms beneath her unresisting body and hefted her more fully onto the bed so that her legs no longer dangled over the side.

"What…?"

"Shh. Just trying to get us both a little more comfortable."

She saw him wince as he settled himself alongside her, and only then did she remember.

"Ohmigod. Your knee!" She attempted to push herself to a sitting position so she could see for herself if he was okay, but he caught her wrists and pinned them gently but firmly over her head. She'd known he was a big man, yet it wasn't until he was over her like this, with her breasts flattened against his chest, that she realized just how large he really was.

He smiled down at her in a way that caused something in her heart to contract. His eyes were hot as they raked her features. "It's not my knee that's bothering me, sweetheart."

He shifted against her, and there it was—the unmistakable thrust of his erection against her hip. Ivy's breath hitched, and delicious memories of their previous encounter swamped her imagination.

"Maybe this time," she murmured, her gaze fastened on his delectable mouth, "you'll let me finish what I started last night."

"I'm counting on it."

He released her wrists and Ivy rolled toward him, gliding a hand up over his chest to his shoulder. She wanted to touch him everywhere. His skin was like hot satin beneath her fingers. Hooking a leg over his thigh, she pressed intimately against him, reveling in the feel of him, hard and pulsing, against the juncture of her thighs. She slid a hand between their bodies and cupped him through the stretchy material of his briefs, loving how he jerked beneath her fingers.

"Oh, my," she murmured appreciatively, and slipped her fingers beneath the waistband to take him in her hand, dragging a little grunt from him.

Garrett dropped his head to her shoulder. "Oh, man," he said raggedly, "that almost feels too good."

Ivy had to agree. He felt incredible in her palm. She

stroked her thumb over the knob of his erection, feeling the slick moisture there.

"I think you have too many clothes on," she whispered, pressing her lips against his chest and flicking her tongue over a nipple. "Can we do something about that?"

"You bet." His response was immediate. He pushed his briefs off and kicked them free. And there he was, as muscular as the rest of him, rising thick and rigid against the flatness of his stomach. Ivy's mouth went dry as she thought of that part of him inside her.

She dragged her gaze upward, forcing herself to look into his eyes. They were as dark as hammered bronze, and turbulent with passion. For her. A primal thrill coursed through her at the raw desire on his face, even as a niggling fear uncoiled itself from somewhere deep within her.

It wasn't a physical fear as much as it was a realization that he was completely different from any man she'd ever been involved with, and she could so easily become addicted to him. Which was crazy. As she'd told herself already, this might be their only time together. They might not have more than these few hours. She knew instinctively that her heart was in danger, but suddenly didn't care. She wanted him. All of him. Any way she could have him. She wouldn't think about what tomorrow might bring, or the day after. He was there with her now, and that was all that mattered.

"I want this so much. But are you sure about this?" she asked. Her voice was almost inaudible.

Garrett gave a strangled laugh. "Sweetheart, when I'm around you, the only thing I *am* sure of is how badly I want you."

This time, there was no question in Ivy's mind that he was talking about her, and her desire for him kicked up a notch. All she could think about was getting closer to him. He took her hand and guided it back to him, and Ivy needed no further incentive to wrap her fingers around him. He pulsed strongly against her palm. God, he was so hot. And hard. And as smooth as satin beneath her fingertips.

She slid her hand down the length of his shaft and felt a surge of possessive pride when he sucked his breath in sharply and then buried his face against her neck. Knowing she affected him so strongly was intoxicating. Ivy continued to stroke him, tentatively at first and then with growing confidence as he groaned softly and bent his head to her breast, capturing her nipple in his mouth and drawing deeply on it.

And there it was again. The throbbing that made her long to wrap her legs around him and bring him completely inside her.

"Garrett," she whispered against his hair, "please…"

He raised his head from her breast and his eyes were startlingly bright. "Yeah?"

"Please, Garrett…I want you. Inside me."

"Ah, sweetheart…I'm all yours. But, damn, I almost forgot." He slanted her a crooked grin and then reached over the edge of the bed to fumble with his discarded jeans. When he came back up, he held a small foil package.

A condom! God, she hadn't even thought about protection. She wondered briefly if he'd had protection when he was with Helena, and then pushed the thought away. She didn't want to think about Helena, and she especially didn't want to think of Helena with Garrett, doing *this*. For tonight, at least, he was all hers.

She watched as he covered himself and positioned himself above her. Then he lifted one of her legs and laid it across his back, opening her for him. He stroked a finger along the cleft of her womanhood and Ivy gasped at the exquisite sensation. Pleasure lashed through her. When she felt the smooth knob of his erection nudging against her, she raised her hips in invitation.

"Do you want me to stop?" His voice was rough, his breathing coming in hard pants. His gaze didn't waver as he stared down at her.

"No. Please, no."

With his eyes fixed on hers, he gave one powerful thrust and buried himself fully in her heat. His possession of her was so total that she almost stopped breathing.

"Oh, God," she whispered, and closed her eyes.

"Look at me," he ordered.

Ivy opened her eyes. He braced himself above her, his expression intense. Then, with their gazes locked on each other, he began to move, pumping hard and deep. Ivy cried out as he filled her, and clutched mindlessly at his shoulders. He captured her mouth with his, sweeping his tongue against hers. His hands cupped her buttocks and lifted her to better meet the bone-melting thrusts of his hips against hers. Ivy arched against him and raised both legs to wrap them around his lean hips.

"That's it," he rasped against her mouth. "You're incredibly tight. Am I hurting you?"

"No," she managed to gasp. "It's just been a while since— You feel so good."

Ivy had never experienced anything so all-consuming. He drove out every conscious thought she had. There was only him, connected to her.

She was being swept upward in a vortex of sensations, clinging helplessly to his shoulders, almost sobbing with the fierceness of her need. He was moving faster now, pumping into her with increasing urgency. He lifted his head to look at her. His features were taut, and a vein pulsed strongly in his neck. He was close to climaxing, and again, knowing that she was responsible was a powerful aphrodisiac. Liquid heat flooded to the spot where he stroked her and heightened the sharpness of her desire.

"Garrett," she cried brokenly, as she felt her own orgasm building again, even more powerful than earlier.

He smoothed the damp tendrils of her hair back from her face. "I'm here," he breathed huskily. "I'm right here with you, babe." He ground his hips against hers, thrusting deeper, until he filled her completely. "I want you to come again."

His words pushed her over the edge.

"Oh, oh," Ivy gasped, and Garrett caught her small, frantic cries with his mouth, tangling his tongue with hers as he moved faster, harder, pushing her higher with each mind-shattering thrust of his hips.

Ivy climaxed in a blinding white-hot rush of pleasure. Garrett bucked against her and gave a harsh cry, and she felt him stiffen and then shudder once, twice and then again, inside her. He collapsed onto her, his breathing hard and fast, and she wrapped her arms around him, not wanting to let him go. She stroked her hands over his back, slick with sweat, and reveled in the feel of his body, heavy and replete against hers.

"Ahh…damn," he gasped, "that was…unbelievable." He raised himself on his elbows over her. He kissed her languorously, but made no move to withdraw from the warmth of her body. When he finally pulled back to look at her, his expression was intensely serious, and filled with a tenderness that made her chest ache. "You okay?"

Ivy gazed at him. "I think so." Her legs were still curved around his hips, and both her and Garrett's breathing was uneven as they stared at each other.

As if unable to help himself, Garrett dipped his head and kissed her again, a kiss so sweet Ivy thought she could willingly stay in his arms like that forever. When he finally lifted his head, it was to carefully withdraw from her body. As he rolled away from her and sat on the edge of the bed to dispose of the condom, she curled on her side and watched him, feeling bereft. She wanted to pull him back against her and absorb his heat and strength. She never wanted to leave his bed.

"I probably shouldn't stay too long," she said without conviction. "It's almost daybreak. People will start talking."

Garrett turned and arched an eyebrow at her, the expression in his eyes telling her he knew how insincere her words were. He stretched back out on the mattress beside her, pulling the sheet over their bodies. Ivy had no time to protest as he drew her back against his body and wrapped his arms completely around her, spooning her against his chest.

"Three days," he said softly against her ear. "That was the deal."

Was he serious? Had she been serious? Ivy found she couldn't think clearly when he was this close. She *had* asked him to give her three days, but she hadn't really had a precise idea of what those three days would entail, except that maybe they'd hook up once or twice during that time.

"Are you saying we'll stay here—in your cabin—for the entire three days?"

He smoothed her hair back behind her ear and nuzzled her neck. His jaw was rough with whiskers and caused delicious shivers of sensation to finger their way across her skin. "You're the one who set the terms, sweetheart." He pressed a lingering kiss to the sensitive area just below her ear, while his big hand brushed over her body, to settle at the juncture of her thighs. "'Three days of no-strings sex.' Your words, not mine."

Ivy laughed uncertainly. "Well, yes, but I thought…I didn't think…" She gave a small groan of frustration and twisted her head to look at him. "You don't really intend for us to be locked together in this room for three days nonstop, do you?"

His grin was swift and appreciative. "Trust me," he said, catching the lobe of her ear lightly between his teeth, while his hand slid between her thighs to explore further, "there's nothing I'd rather do."

He pressed his hips meaningfully against her, and there he was, hot and hard once more, against her buttocks and ready for round two. But instead of pressuring her to accept him, he pulled away from her and lay back against the pillows, arms bent beneath his head.

Curious, Ivy peered at him over her shoulder. In the indistinct light, he was all sculpted muscles and bare skin, and almost against her will, she found herself turning to face him. Of its own volition, her hand reached out and traced the hard ridges of his stomach, then lower to where his arousal begged for her touch. She enclosed him in her hand, feeling him pulse beneath her fingers.

"Oh, yeah," he murmured. "See what you do to me? Just thinking about you makes me hard. And when you touch me—" He gave a self-deprecating laugh. "Christ. Three days of this might kill me."

Unable to help herself, Ivy laughed. "I won't let that happen. I'm your guardian angel, remember?" She dropped a kiss on his shoulder. "Besides, I don't want to disappoint Finn with some mediocre love scenes. You'd better show me everything."

Garrett grinned, a slow, wicked grin of promise. "With pleasure."

9

SHE WAS WARM, AND MORE comfortable than she could remember being in a long time. With a soft sigh, she snuggled deeper into the cocoon that surrounded her. She was dreaming, a sensual dream of exploration that slowly aroused her and had her seeking more. Hands smoothed over her body, soothing and exciting at the same time. She stretched languorously, practically purring with contentment, and shifted to get closer to the source of the wonderful contact. Her breasts pressed against something hard. But when a callused hand skated along the length of her bare thigh, then lifted her leg to settle it across hips that were unmistakably male in their hardness, her eyes flew open.

This was no dream.

She found herself staring into eyes the shade of dark honey, drowsy with sleep and the beginnings of sexual awareness. Daylight streamed through the windows, penetrating the gossamer netting that surrounded them, gilding his skin with sunlight.

Gradually, she realized her breasts were indeed pressed against the muscled hardness of Garrett's body and one leg was draped over his hips. She could feel him, hard and hot, against the juncture of her thighs. For a moment, she couldn't move, couldn't even breathe. She could only stare into his eyes. The blackness of his pupils almost drowned out the hammered bronze of his irises.

Then, slowly, as if in a dream, he slid his hand down over the curve of her buttock. He briefly cupped the firm mound before his hand moved lower, dipped between her legs, and his fingers found the most intimate part of her. As he drew his fingers along her cleft, her breath caught and then shuddered softly out.

How long had they slept? Had it been hours—or minutes—since they'd last made love? Her body felt sated and deliciously sore in places she hadn't even known existed, but as his fingers found her center, moisture swamped her and desire laced through her. She gave a ragged sigh of surrender and pushed closer to him, sliding her own hand over the flat hardness of his stomach, feeling the ridges of muscle contract beneath her fingers.

He growled approvingly, and his fingers tormented her slick flesh as he gently circled a finger over her clitoris. She moaned and pushed against his hand, wanting more of the delicious sensations that caused a sensual heat to build between her legs.

How was it this guy had the ability to arouse her so quickly? Or so easily? Maybe it had something to do with the languorous pace he set, as if they had all the time in the world, despite the fact his own arousal was more than apparent.

Without a word, Garrett caught her mouth with his, feasting on her lips. She ran her hands up over his shoulders, marveling anew at their width and strength. Her hands moved over the hard muscles of his back, reveling in the smooth rise and fall of bone and sinew. But then her fingers encountered a ridge of scar tissue near his hip. Her exploration stilled. How had she not noticed this earlier? Was it another gunshot wound? A knife to the back, perhaps?

How many scars could one body carry? How many times had his life been threatened? She'd asked him to help her with the love scenes, but the realization hit her that this was no actor she held in her arms. He wasn't Bruce Willis or Vin Diesel, who took one punishing blow after another and still managed to overcome the bad guy and walk away; this was a real man who had put himself in real peril and suffered real injuries as a result.

"What is this from?" she asked, gently probing the damaged flesh. "Another bullet wound?"

He reached behind him, pulled her hands away from his back and stretched them over her head. "Shrapnel," he murmured, pressing warm, insistent kisses against her skin. "Got me just below my vest. It was no big deal."

No big deal? Ivy felt as though she'd been doused with cold water. She couldn't believe he could be so cavalier about something that might have killed him, that *had* killed countless other soldiers. Soldiers like her brother, who hadn't been so lucky. She struggled briefly against Garrett's hold on her.

"How many times have you been injured?" she asked, hating how her voice broke. "How many times has somebody tried to kill you?"

He lifted his head to look at her, and as he searched her face, something flashed in his eyes. Comprehension. Remorse. Sympathy.

"Aw, shit," he muttered, and rolled to his side, pulling her with him and hugging her to his chest. "I'm sorry, babe. I wasn't thinking. I forgot…you lost a brother."

"You—you know about my brother?" Her voice was muffled against his shoulder.

He hesitated, then bestowed a kiss on her temple. "Yeah. Iraq, right?"

She nodded before easing back to consider him. "How do you know about him?"

Garrett hesitated, then raised her hand and placed his mouth against her palm. "Finn does a complete background check on every actor," he finally said, entwining his fingers with hers. "When he realized your brother was in the service, he mentioned it to me, since obviously it's something I'd relate to."

"Oh."

His arm tightened around her. "It must've been rough for you."

"Devon was all I had left." She cleared her throat at the constriction there, willing herself not to cry, but she couldn't stop the tightness in her chest that always accompanied her memories of her brother. "My dad died in a car accident when we were both in elementary school, and Mom was diagnosed with cancer while Devon was serving his second tour of Iraq." Ivy bit her lip at the memory. "He didn't make it back in time to say goodbye to her. It really bothered him."

"I'm sorry. That must have been tough on your mom, raising two kids alone. Were you close to her?"

Ivy smiled at the memory of her exuberant, free-spirited mother. "Oh, yeah. Losing my dad was really hard for her, but I think it just made her more determined to live her life to the fullest. When I wanted to ditch college and head straight to Hollywood, she didn't try to stop me. She simply reminded me that some of the best actors also had undergraduate degrees. And she didn't try to talk Devon out of enlisting in the marines, either, even though she didn't agree with the war."

Garrett hugged her tighter and pressed another kiss to her temple. "She sounds like a special lady. I'm sure she was very proud of you."

"She used to have these big, crazy parties for me whenever one of my movies came out, even if it was a box-office flop. She always had so much faith in me. I think that's part of the reason getting cast for this role means so much to me. It's like I'm not letting her down." Ivy twisted her face to look at him. "What about you? Do you have family?"

Garrett laughed. "Oh, yeah. I have four older sisters, and my folks are still alive and well in northern California."

"Four sisters? Wow."

Garrett chuckled. "Yep. My mom always wanted a son, and she wasn't about to stop until she got one."

Ivy laughed. "I guess you're lucky you only have four sisters, then."

"Trust me," he said wryly, "four was enough. They used to dress me up like a little girl—at least, until I got old enough to outrun them. It's probably one of the reasons I joined the military. I felt like I had something to prove. At any rate, I'm sorry about the loss of your brother. I didn't mean to upset you."

Ivy drew in a deep breath. "It's okay. I guess it's just…seeing your wounds brings everything back." She met his eyes. "Even reading the script and knowing you really had to go through all those horrors doesn't make it as real as—as seeing your scars does."

If anything, her scars made her realize how lucky he'd been to survive, and how fortunate she was to be holding him, warm and alive, in her arms. Two weeks ago, she hadn't even known Garrett Stokes existed. But now that she knew…she couldn't even think about the possibility of him being killed and not have a shudder go through her.

"Hey." He cupped her face, staring down at her. "I'm okay. I survived."

"I know, but—"

"If I hadn't had those experiences, I wouldn't be here, holding you." He searched her eyes. "If being tortured and shot and hunted like an animal in the jungle was the price I had to pay to be here with you, I'd do it all again in a heartbeat."

Ivy's breath caught. There was no mistaking the sincerity of his words, but a part of her couldn't help but wonder whom he was talking to—her or Helena? She wasn't even certain she wanted to know. For now, it was enough that he was here, with her.

"So here's the thing," he said, his voice a little rough. "I really want to make love to you again, but if you're not up to it...if I repel you somehow—"

She lifted her head and pressed a swift kiss to his lips, interrupting his words. Pulling back, she covered his hand where it still cradled her face and slowly drew it downward until it covered her breast, then watched in fascination as his eyes darkened.

"It's not too much," she assured him. "And there's nothing repellent about you, as you very well know. In fact, I need..."

"What?" A whisper of air was all that separated his lips from hers. "What do you need?"

"You," she breathed, and closed the infinitesimal space to cover his mouth with her own. Slipping her arms under his, she edged nearer, wanting to absorb him, to surround him and keep him close to her, as if by doing so, she could prevent him from ever being hurt again.

He slanted his mouth over hers and she opened for

him, welcoming the sweet intrusion of his tongue against her own. She lost track of how long they kissed, long and deep, while their hands roamed freely over each other. She stroked her palms over his back and lower, to grasp his firm buttocks and pull him against her hips.

"Oh, man," he groaned, "see what you do to me."

His erection throbbed against her belly, stiff and begging to be touched. Ivy complied, wrapping him in her hand and stroking him until his breathing changed, became shallow and ragged. Easing back, she watched his face as passion drew it taut and turned his eyes to molten bronze. Her response to him was just as strong. Heat coiled low in her womb, and she knew that if he was to touch her, she'd be slick and wet.

He shifted and prepared to pull her beneath him, but Ivy stopped him with a hand on his chest. He raised his head, his eyes smoky.

"What?"

"Not like this," she whispered, and pushed against the solid planes of his chest until he lay on his back beneath her. "Like this…"

She straddled his thighs, scooting back just enough that she could still touch him freely. She continued to stroke him, greedily devouring him with her eyes, reveling as he responded to her touch.

"Ah, babe," he ground out, "you're so damn beautiful."

He trailed his hands over her thighs and along her flanks, tested the curve of her hips and buttocks, before smoothing over her belly to cup her breasts. He played with her nipples, plucking them and rolling them between his fingers until they were flushed and distended.

The sight of his strong hands on her pale body was intensely erotic, and Ivy couldn't help rubbing herself against his thigh even as her hands continued to stroke him.

"That's it," he rasped. "Ride me."

Her breathing quickened as she ground herself against the hard muscle of his leg. With one hand fisted around him, she stroked his sac, loving the way his entire body tightened. A drop of glistening moisture eased from the blunt head of his erection, and Ivy caught it with her thumb, smoothing it over the sensitized skin beneath until he groaned and thrust against her. His hands kneaded her breasts, then slid down to cup her buttocks and tip her off balance, so that she fell forward onto his chest.

"Oh, yeah," he breathed, and slipped a hand between her buttocks to stroke her from behind, even as he caught her mouth with his and drew deeply on her tongue.

He captured her muffled cry of pleasure with his mouth, and his fingers slid into her slick heat, stroking and circling until she thought she'd explode if he didn't fill her completely.

"Can't—I can't wait," she panted.

Without breaking the delicious torment of his fingers, he reached over his head to where he'd stashed a handful of condoms earlier, grabbed one and tore its package with his teeth. He spat the corner out, then, with shaking hands, covered himself with the condom.

Ivy watched, amazed and more than a little humbled that she could have such an effect on him. But then she realized she was trembling, too.

She didn't have time to think about it. He gripped her hips and guided her into position. Then there was no more thought as she slid down over him, feeling him stretching and filling her. Bracing one hand on his chest, she used her thighs to leverage herself up and down, watching his features tighten as he watched her.

He gripped her buttocks as she rocked, and the combination of having him inside her while his hands squeezed and stroked her was almost unbearable. She didn't want to come yet, wanted to hold off and prolong her pleasure, to drive him to the point where he felt the same desperate need she was feeling.

"Ah...sweetheart," he rasped. "I'm not going to last when you move like that."

"Okay," she said breathlessly, "how's this, instead?"

Pushing herself upright, she arched her back so that her breasts thrust forward, and then she ran her hands along her rib cage and cupped her breasts, pinching her nipples as she watched Garrett's face.

He groaned, and his fingers flexed against her, but he didn't try to take over, just fixed her with an expression of rapt intensity and raw, male appreciation in his eyes. Ivy had never felt so powerful or beautiful, and it all had to do with the way he looked at her.

Well, that and the incredible sensations he was creating with the friction of his body against hers. She moaned softly and raised her arms, thrusting her fingers through her hair and biting her lip as an orgasm began to build deep within her.

"Oh...I'm going to come," she gasped, feeling her inner muscles begin to clench around him.

Her words dragged a rough sound of need from Garrett, who thrust upward at just the right angle, so that wave after undulating wave of intense pleasure washed over her. Her vision blurred, but she was aware of Garrett tensing beneath her, the cords in his neck standing out sharply, before he thrust one last time, the force of his release wrenching a harsh cry from him.

Ivy collapsed against his chest, feeling boneless and weak. His hands caressed her back, then trailed along her spine to rest on the cheeks of her butt. She clenched her muscles, enjoying how they were still joined.

"What a way to wake up," she said, breathless.

"No shit," he agreed, his voice caught between a laugh and a groan. "I may never leave this bed again, just sleep and…wake up, over and over."

Ivy smiled and traced her lips along the column of his neck. He tasted salty and spicy at the same time, his skin warm beneath her mouth.

"Mmm…you taste good," she murmured.

"Which reminds me," he said, giving her bottom a playful slap and setting her gently but firmly away from him. "I'm starving. You?"

Ivy shrugged and smiled. "Sort of. I don't know. I mean, what did you have in mind?"

Garrett stood, and she pulled the sheet over her nudity and watched him. He kept a pitcher and bowl on the counter near the door, and now he splashed some water onto a cloth and quickly washed up. It was the first time she'd gotten a really good look at his entire body, and it just about took her breath away. Garrett Stokes in the buff wasn't just attractive; he was incredibly, darkly, dangerously gorgeous. His shoulders were wide and powerful, and she admired the play of muscles through his arms and along his back as he moved.

With the sun slanting in through the windows, she could also better see the scars that marred the perfection of his physique, pale splotches and slashes that caused her heart to tighten.

"Are you still with Special Ops?" She realized she knew so little about this man, other than what she'd read in the script. "I mean, are you still active duty?"

He squeezed out the excess water from the cloth and laid it on the counter next to the washbasin. "Yeah," he finally responded. "I'm stationed at Fort Bragg."

"Oh." Ivy digested this news in silence, then tipped her head and considered him. "They let you wear your hair long? I thought all military guys had to get the basic buzz cut."

Garrett gave her a swift grin and shrugged. "Well, Special Forces and Special Ops can pretty much grow their hair however they need to in order to blend in with the local population or gain the acceptance of indigenous fighters."

"So does that mean you still do covert-ops stuff, like you did in Colombia?"

He didn't answer right away. Instead, he drew a pair of clean cargo pants from the shelving unit next to the bed and yanked them on. Ivy noticed the muscles along his rib cage flex and tighten with his movements.

"I'm an instructor at Fort Bragg's Special Warfare School," he replied at last, pulling up the zipper and fastening the button. "They have a qualification course called SERE—Survival, Evasion, Resistance and Escape." A brief smile touched his mouth. "My superior officers decided I'm more than qualified to teach any or all of the four segments of the course."

Ivy had learned enough about the military from her brother to know that Fort Bragg was an enormous army base in North Carolina, and was where the closely guarded training center for the Special Operations Command was located. Devon had hoped to someday qualify for the Special Forces training program.

"So you're on leave right now?"

"Yes and no. The army considers this a public-relations opportunity," Garrett said drily. He picked up the basin and, opening the screen door with his hip, tossed the contents outside onto the ground. He placed the empty bowl back on the counter, which he leaned against, considering her. "I'm on special assignment. As a technical consultant for the filming, my job is to ensure that Finn and the movie producers depict the events as accurately as possible, without giving away any military secrets or compromising a mission."

Ivy pushed herself to a sitting position and wrapped her arms around her knees. She loved listening to Garrett talk. She hugged her knees, happier and more content than she could remember being in a very long time. As she listened to Garrett, it struck her that she was in danger of falling completely and ridiculously in love with the man. She was half-there already.

She never wanted to leave his cabin. She knew he had feelings for her, too, but didn't know if they were strong enough to last beyond this idyllic interlude. Had his interest in her been no more than role-playing? No, she couldn't believe that. He'd been too completely involved, both with his mind and his body, for it to have been acting. She wanted it to be real. She wanted to forget about Helena and the film, and have him see her for who she was—Ivy James. Not a stand-in, not an actress, just a woman who was falling hard for him.

"So when this is over you'll…what? Go back to Fort Bragg and continue teaching?" He'd said he was permanently stationed at the army base. Did that mean he no longer went out of the country on dangerous missions? She knew the injury to his leg probably prevented him from doing the things he'd done before the events in Colombia. It was selfish of her, but she fervently hoped his days of conducting covert operations were over.

"Yep. What about you? Any projects lined up after this one?"

Ivy didn't miss how abruptly he'd changed the subject. "No. In fact, if this one hadn't turned up when it did, I'd be out of work right now." She rested her cheek on her knees. "It was actually a little bizarre how this job arrived completely out of the blue. When I found out the rest of the cast was already here, *had* been here for several weeks...well, it made me wonder."

Garrett stilled. "What did it make you wonder?"

"Just...I don't know...why a director like Finn Mac-Dougall would want to cast me in the lead female role." She gave a huff of laughter. "He could have had anyone he wanted. I've never won any awards, and none of my films has been a huge hit. Finn's never told me what made him cast me, so while I'd like to think it's because he appreciates my talent, I'm just not sure."

"You don't give yourself enough credit," Garrett said gruffly. "You got some great reviews for your portrayal of that schoolteacher in *The Red Fence*."

"You saw that?" Ivy couldn't keep the surprise out of her voice. Of all her roles, that one had been her favorite. She also thought it had been her most powerful role to date, although *Eye of the Hunter* had all the makings of a huge box-office hit—*if* she could nail Helena's character the way Finn wanted. But *The Red Fence* had been relatively obscure, and its distribution hadn't been wide. "Have you seen any of my other films?"

"Maybe a few." Garrett pushed himself away from the counter. "I asked Josephina to bring some food out to us, and I'm sure I heard her outside a few minutes ago. Be right back."

Without waiting for Ivy's response, he opened the

screen door and was gone, leaving her to stare after him in bemusement. She couldn't dispel the distinct feeling that he'd used the food as an excuse to avoid further discussion of her films. The thing she couldn't figure out was *why?*

_10_

GARRETT KNEW HE WAS in real trouble. As a Special Forces soldier, he'd been ready for all types of conventional and clandestine warfare, but nothing could have prepared him for the effect this one woman had on him. He'd been more than a little infatuated with her before he'd ever met her, and that was just from the info he'd gathered about her through public—and not so public—resources. But the real, living, breathing, in-your-arms Ivy James completely blew him away.

He'd had some insane idea that maybe—just maybe—sleeping with her would tamp down the lust that roiled through his blood each time he saw her.

Now he knew differently.

He'd had her a half-dozen times over the course of the forty-eight hours they'd been together in his little cabin and the truth was, he wanted her more than ever. It was as if he couldn't get enough of her. As if his body had been on hold the past two years, hoarding all the passion he had for her, so that even now, when they'd made love to the point where they were both tender and aching, it still didn't make a dent in the stockpile he had remaining.

It scared the hell out of him. He'd never felt this way, and a part of him wasn't sure whether his feelings for Ivy were real or merely a by-product of the exotic location and the film they were shooting. Ivy, on the other hand, seemed completely unfazed by any of it. She made love to him as sweetly and wholeheartedly as if she really was in love with him. He acknowledged that it wouldn't take much for him to believe they could actually make a go of a relationship. A real relationship, with a real commitment.

They were lying together in his hammock, watching the sun sink over the mountains in a ball of red-gold brilliance, while Garrett peeled an orange and fed Ivy slices of the succulent fruit.

"Mmm," she murmured, biting into a wedge and trying unsuccessfully to keep it from dribbling down her chin. "It's delicious—but too juicy!"

Garrett bent his head and caught the excess juice with his tongue, licking it from her chin and then following the trail to her lips, where he licked some more, before kissing her thoroughly. She tasted like sweet citrus, and she smelled like his soap and shampoo. They'd showered together behind his cabin, where a cistern on the roof caught rainwater for the primitive outdoor shower he'd rigged up just after he'd arrived. Normally, he wouldn't have even bothered with a curtain, but he hadn't wanted to risk anyone seeing Ivy, so he'd strung a tarp around the perimeter of the shower.

He recalled again how hot she'd looked in the shadowy interior, with the cool rainwater sluicing over her sleek body. He'd taken his time washing her hair, working his fingers along her scalp before rinsing it. He'd been surprised at just how long her hair was when it was straight. He'd run his hands over the slick length and then lower, along the smooth skin of her back, feeling her shoulder blades thrust against his palms before he'd filled his hands with her buttocks and lifted her. She'd cried out once, in surprise, as he'd pinned her against the wall of the cabin, and then once more, in pleasure, as he'd entered her. Then there had been no sounds at all as their mouths had fused and she'd ridden him, hard and fast, to completion.

That had been less than two hours ago and yet now, kissing her, he could feel his body tightening once more in arousal. Ivy wore her bathrobe and nothing else, and Garrett couldn't resist slipping his hand beneath the silken material to mold her breast. He deepened the kiss, exploring the sweet recesses of her mouth and loving how she responded, instantly and without reservations.

He dragged his mouth from hers, but didn't stop the slow exploration of her satiny skin. "We can't do this," he said, his voice sounding rough.

"Why not?" She slid her hand over his abdomen and lower, to where his arousal pressed against the front of his cargo pants. "It seems to me you're more than ready."

"Ready and willing," he groaned, "but somebody's coming down the path."

Without giving her time to protest, he withdrew his arm from beneath her shoulders and swung his legs over the edge of the hammock to the ground. Assuring himself that Ivy was covered, he stood, easing the stiffness from his bad leg. He'd heard footsteps on the path that led from the hacienda to his *casita,* but he was unprepared for the man who finally emerged from the dense foliage.

"Whoa, Finn!" he exclaimed, unable to keep the surprise out of his voice. "What are you doing back?"

What the hell *was* he doing back so early? By Garrett's estimation, Finn and the film crew—and Eric Terrell—should have been gone for at least another twenty-four hours.

Finn's eyes swept beyond Garrett to the hammock, where Ivy was oh-so-casually trying to push her robe down lower over her legs.

Garrett knew and trusted Finn enough to feel confident that whatever he might personally think about seeing Garrett and Ivy together, he wouldn't so much as mention it to anyone else. But for an instant, he thought he saw disappointment in the other man's eyes. Then it was gone, and Garrett wasn't certain if what he'd seen was real or just a figment of his imagination.

"We, ah, wrapped up the jungle shoot this afternoon," Finn said, shifting his gaze back to Garrett. "I'd like you to watch the dailies with me, help me spot any technical problems."

"Absolutely." Reviewing the film clips from the last two days could take hours, but the process was essential in evaluating performance and detecting any issues that could have a negative impact on the final product. Inwardly, however, every curse he knew—and he knew plenty—was rolling viciously through his head. He cursed Finn's bad timing; he cursed the fact that he hadn't figured this exact scenario into his plans; and he cursed himself for not taking better care of Ivy's reputation. Instead, he'd allowed her to be caught in what was unquestionably a compromising situation. He pinched the bridge of his nose. "Give me about fifteen minutes, would you? I want to walk Ivy back to the hacienda, then I'll be right there."

"Actually," Finn said smoothly, "I wanted to speak to Ivy, too."

Garrett glanced at Ivy, who was struggling to sit upright and look composed as the flimsy netting of the hammock threatened to unseat her completely. Reaching back, he caught her hand and pulled her to her feet.

He had to give her credit. She tightened the belt of her robe, smoothed a hand over the unruly mass of her hair and smiled as if completely comfortable.

"Hey, Finn. It's good to see you back." She glanced swiftly at Garrett and then back at the director. "I want you to know that I—I took your advice to heart, and I hope you'll be pleased with how I intend to interpret the love scenes."

Finn arched one bushy eyebrow. "So I take it you found your inspiration?"

"Well," she began, "I asked Garrett to give me a few pointers. You know…share his experiences with me so that I could gain a better understanding of what transpired between him and—and my character."

Finn's eyebrow rose fractionally higher. *"Really."* He shot Garrett a look that said clearly what Garrett was already thinking: he was a total and complete scumbag.

"We didn't follow the script to the letter," Ivy continued. "We improvised. But I feel I have a better understanding of how to approach the love scenes."

"Improvised, huh?" Finn sounded less than enthusiastic.

Ivy actually smiled. "Yes. If you recall, Eric recommended that, and in retrospect, I feel it was an excellent suggestion."

"Excellent," Finn repeated dully. Garrett knew the other man well enough to guess the direction of his thoughts; he believed Ivy was going to completely botch tomorrow's shoot. Finn sighed deeply and handed her a slip of paper. "You'll have an opportunity to demonstrate your newfound techniques tomorrow morning. Here's your call sheet. We'll reshoot the love scenes beginning at 8:00 a.m., so I suggest you get a good night's sleep."

Which meant that Ivy would need to report to hair and makeup by 5:30 or 6:00 a.m., which meant he really did need to walk her back to her room so she could get some sleep. God knew she hadn't gotten much in the past forty-eight hours.

"Thanks, Finn," he said. "I'll be along in a few minutes."

After the other man had left, Garrett turned to Ivy. She had her arms wrapped around her middle, and for an instant, she looked vulnerable. But as he watched her, it was like seeing a shutter close over an open window. Her expression became studiously composed and she smiled politely at him, as if they were strangers and hadn't spent the past two days plastered against each other.

"Well," she said, her voice bright. "I guess this is it, huh? My so-called acting lessons are officially over. I just want to—to thank you for everything you did."

Garrett stepped forward so that he was right there in her space. Apart from one swift indrawn breath, she gave no indication that his closeness affected her.

"Three days," he said softly, searching her eyes. "That was the deal."

He saw, with satisfaction, that her eyes widened. "But…that was when we thought the film crew would be gone for three days. Just because they're back a day early—"

Garrett slid a hand beneath the fall of her hair. Her nape was warm against his fingers. "Three days," he repeated, massaging her silky skin. "I don't care when it happens, but I insist on having everything you promised, and that was three days of—"

"No-strings sex," she finished for him. "Yes, I remember."

"You can't tell me you won't be looking forward to one more day," he insisted softly. "In fact, I'm certain that if Finn and the rest of the crew never returned, you'd be okay with that."

He noticed that she swallowed hard and for an instant her eyes shifted away from him. "Maybe," she finally conceded.

Garrett laughed. "I'm right, and you know it."

That wrung a reluctant smile out of her, but she refused to agree with him. "Finn's waiting for you, and I have to go back to my room."

"I'll walk you." He captured her hand in his, linking their fingers. He liked how she leaned into him as they made their way back along the path that led to the hacienda, as though she needed him. As though she trusted him. Having her beside him like this felt incredibly right, and he realized with a growing sense of dismay that he already thought of her as his.

His woman.

He didn't believe their two days together had been nothing more than meaningless sex, either. Garrett would bet his last peso on the fact that at some point during that time, she'd made a connection with him on more than just a physical level. She genuinely liked being with him, and that was good enough for him.

For now.

Before the filming was through, he'd make sure she liked him a whole lot more. He may have started their relationship under less than truthful conditions, but his long-term intentions toward her were completely honorable. The past two days had firmly cemented just one thought into his head: he wanted Ivy in his life for the long haul.

They approached the rear entrance to the hacienda, and Ivy pulled him to a halt on the dimly lit path.

"What's wrong?"

She glanced at the hacienda, with its illuminated court-yard and balconies. "You don't have to walk me to my room. I'll be fine from here, and Finn's waiting for you."

Garrett followed her gaze toward the courtyard, where he could make out several shadowy figures on a second-floor balcony. She didn't want anyone seeing them together, especially when she wore nothing more than a silky bathrobe.

"Okay, fine. I'll just wait here until you're inside."

She nodded and pulled her hand free from his grasp. "Okay. Thanks."

She didn't try to kiss him good-night, but she didn't seem in a hurry to leave, either. Garrett bent his head down to look into her eyes. "What's wrong?"

"Can I, um, ask you a personal question?"

"Sure."

He waited as she struggled for words, twisting the sash of her robe in her hands. "I just want to know—what is your relationship with Helena now? I mean, it's been more than two years since—since it all happened. Do you still see her?"

Garrett hesitated. He should just tell her the truth about Helena. She'd be as mad as hell, and he wouldn't blame her, but he'd make it up to her. But he also knew that now wasn't the time to come clean. She had a big shoot to do in the morning, a shoot that could either make or break her role as a lead character in the movie. Telling her the truth now might jeopardize her ability to focus on her job. He knew how important it was to her that she impress Finn, and he wouldn't do anything to ruin that. He might not be able to tell her the whole truth, but he could tell her a partial truth.

He blew out his breath. "Well, here's the thing…"

His voice sounded gruff even to his own ears. "I haven't seen her since I was airlifted out of Colombia. She sent me a get-well card while I was in the hospital, and I got a Christmas card from her that first year, but since then…nothing."

Ivy was silent for a long moment, and he sensed her dismay at this news. She'd thought he and Helena were an item; that they were still together.

"Did you try to stay in touch with her?"

Garrett shrugged. "Sure. I sent her a letter once I returned to the States, and she sent me the Christmas card, but after that…well, there wasn't much point in continuing our…relationship. She wasn't leaving her mission in Colombia and I wasn't going back. The chances of our even seeing each other again were pretty remote."

Ivy studied her hands. When she finally looked at him, her expression was carefully neutral. "I see."

Garrett arched an eyebrow. "Do you?"

"I've heard," she began carefully, "that sometimes when two people are forced to coexist under extreme conditions or when their very survival is threatened, they can form a short-term, intense relationship that usually doesn't last beyond the period of endangerment."

"That's right," he agreed. "There's a third *F* to the 'Fight or Flight' theory that no one mentions."

"Right." She cleared her throat. "It's just survival sex, or end-of-the-world sex."

"Out-of-this-world sex, you mean," he murmured, thinking of the past two days.

"What?"

"I just meant that I agree. When your life is in danger and you don't know if you're going to survive, you want to reaffirm your own existence. To say, 'I'm alive, I'm functioning.' And let's face it, sex is the deepest physical closeness. It's basic in the most biological sense. There's no more obvious antidote to death than sex."

Ivy was silent for a long moment, and Garrett would have given anything to know what was going through her head.

"So what are the chances that you'll see her again?"

"Helena?" Garrett shrugged. "Like you said—it's been more than two years. If I haven't seen her once in all that time, there's a strong likelihood I'll never see her again."

He couldn't tell if relief or censure made her briefly close her eyes, but when she opened them again, her expression was carefully composed.

"Well, I guess as long as neither one of you had expectations of something long-term or permanent, then there's no harm done, yes?"

"Absolutely. I can say with one-hundred-percent certainty that neither of us had any such expectations."

She nodded and tucked a loose spiral of hair behind one ear, her eyes sliding away from his. "Well, I should probably let you go…to Finn."

"Yeah. Okay. So I'll see you tomorrow, then. On the set. And, Ivy, these past two days—"

"It's okay," she said, interrupting him. "You don't have to say anything. I don't regret any of it." Her lips curved in a quick smile. "In fact, I should probably thank you."

"For what?"

"Well, let's just say I'll approach tomorrow's shoot with a whole new perspective. A whole new attitude, in fact. Wait until you see." She gave him a smile that was both sweet and sexy and made Garrett want to haul her against him and kiss her senseless. Instead, he watched as she turned and walked through the arched gateway to the interior courtyard. Her hands were thrust into the pockets of her bathrobe and pulled the fabric taut across her curvy butt. He loved watching her; he just wished he wasn't watching her walk away, leaving him with the distinct feeling that he wasn't going to be crazy about tomorrow's shoot. Nope, not one bit.

11

IVY STOOD ON THE SIDE of the set and nursed a glass of fruit juice as the lighting technicians fine-tuned their equipment. She'd spent the better part of the day on the set, waiting to shoot the love scene. The filming had been delayed due to various technical problems, and they were hours behind schedule. But rather than reschedule the shoot for the following day, Finn had requested that the actors remain on the set until the problems were fixed. He'd had lunch brought in. Ivy had lounged in her dressing room, flipping through magazines and chatting with Carla.

Long after she'd left Garrett at the entrance to the hacienda, she'd lain awake in bed, replaying every delicious moment of the past two days. They'd taken on a surreal quality, as if she'd only dreamed them. But Garrett's words had been too real, and no matter how she tried, she couldn't forget what he'd said.

He hadn't seen Helena since he'd left Colombia.

She shouldn't be surprised. The script didn't imply that they'd ridden off into the sunset together. In fact, the movie ended with them saying their goodbyes as he was being loaded into a military rescue helicopter. But according to the screenplay, he'd made a promise to Helena that he would return to Colombia. For her.

That hadn't happened.

Ivy should be relieved. While she could tell herself that she and Garrett had been reenacting the time he'd spent with Helena in order for Ivy to film the love scenes more realistically, Ivy knew his attraction to her was genuine. Whatever he'd shared with Helena had been over for a long time, and the passion he'd shown Ivy during the past two days hadn't been an act. No man could have that kind of physical response to a woman unless she completely turned him on.

Yet instead of being relieved, Ivy felt inexplicably sad. The reality was that Garrett Stokes had walked away—figuratively speaking—from Helena Vanderveer. And now, it seemed that even after spending two intensely intimate days together, Garrett Stokes would likely walk away from her, too. When all was said and done, she was just another interlude in his life, enjoyed and then quickly forgotten.

The entire experience had a depressingly familiar feel to it. She closed her eyes briefly in self-disgust. At least this time, Garrett wasn't the leading man. Well, at least not technically.

Ivy wasn't ignorant of how cruel the tabloids could be, and she knew it was only her own relative obscurity as an actor that kept her failed relationships from being publicly raked through the muck.

Hollywood didn't get any more voyeuristic than those movies that aroused passionate, offscreen love affairs. She'd seen what Julia Roberts, Meg Ryan and countless other female actors had endured when sparks had flown more furiously offscreen than on. She should be grateful that Garrett had been discreet, and that aside from Finn and the housekeeper, virtually no one knew that their relationship extended beyond a professional acquaintanceship.

But her self-talk and rationalizations hadn't been enough to keep him from invading her thoughts. In her wide, empty bed, she'd tossed and turned the entire night. As tired as she was, she should have welcomed an uninterrupted night of sleep, but instead she'd found herself unable to close her eyes without vivid images of him intruding into her thoughts.

Alone in her bed, she'd missed him. Ached for him. She'd even gone to the window and leaned on the sill to stare out into the darkness of the night toward his cabin. Was he awake? Did he think of her? Or had he gone to sleep without any trouble?

She'd finally given up any pretense of trying to sleep and had turned on her bedside lamp. Curled up against the pillows, she'd read and reread the entire script in an effort to connect more closely to her character and to understand the main characters' relationships to each other. But each time, her imagination had been swamped with vivid memories of being with Garrett. Of making love to him, of laughing with him, of lying in his arms and listening to him. The pleasure had been tempered by the bittersweet knowledge that their time together would soon be ending.

By the time dawn came, she knew instinctively what she needed to do. When she acted out the love scenes, she would pretend it really was Garrett she was with…Garrett she was in love with…and Garrett who would soon be leaving her life.

The warehouse where the set had been constructed and where the mission scenes were filmed was nearly a mile from the hacienda itself. A driver had collected her and several other cast members from the lobby and driven them to the location in a small, beat-up bus. There had been little conversation during the short ride.

Her eyes ached and she felt slightly sick from lack of sleep. The love scene required that she look tired and fragile, as if she'd gone two days without rest. For Carla to achieve that effect hadn't been difficult. She'd commented on the faint shadows beneath Ivy's eyes, but Ivy had just shrugged and blamed them on the change in weather.

Now, standing on the side of the set and watching the technicians prepare for the scene, she wondered if Garrett would make an appearance. She almost thought it might be easier if he didn't show up. He'd distracted her so much the last time here that she'd been completely unable to focus on her acting.

"So did you miss me?"

The words were spoken softly in her ear, startling her so much that she sloshed orange juice over her hand.

"Oh!" Stepping back, she found herself looking into Eric Terrell's blue eyes. She hadn't heard him approach. In a disconcerting reminder of their encounter by the pool, he wore nothing more than a towel wrapped around his lean hips, and she couldn't help but gape for an instant at all his bare flesh.

She jerked her gaze quickly upward, but not before she'd made a swift, mental comparison of his body to Garrett's and decided there was simply no comparison. As beautiful and perfect as Eric's physique was, it couldn't hold a candle to the unabashed masculinity of Garrett's, scars and all.

Eric was so close she could smell the greasepaint that had been used on his body to create the realistic bruises that darkened his jaw and cheekbones, and her first instinct was to step back and put some space between her and him. For an instant she wondered if he would still be piqued with her about their last disastrous shoot, but he seemed totally at ease. He'd never mentioned their nocturnal encounter by the swimming pool, which made her think maybe Garrett was right and Eric didn't remember it. She felt herself relax slightly. No way did she want to start this next shoot with any animosity between them. If he could start fresh, then so could she.

"How did the shoot in Xalapa go?"

"Without a hitch." He gave her a quick wink. "But I have to say I'm just as happy to be back in civilization. Relatively speaking, of course."

She blinked at his friendly tone. Since the first time they'd met, he'd treated her with a kind of sneering superiority, as if he only tolerated her presence in his movie and didn't really consider her an equal. But looking at him now, Ivy thought she saw something like appreciation in his eyes.

She pushed a loose strand of hair back from her forehead and smiled. "That's great. I think we're going to have a good shoot today, too."

Eric's eyes swept over her, and despite the fact that a pair of khaki pants and a button-down shirt completely covered her, she felt as if he was mentally undressing her. It was all she could do not to cross her arms over her breasts.

"Yeah, I think today's shoot will go well, too." He leaned forward and braced a hand against the wall behind her head, effectively trapping her. "But if things start to get too intense, just remember it's only my acting method. I told you before that I tend to really get into character, but it's nothing personal, okay?"

Ivy continued to smile at him, although inwardly she wondered if this was his way of apologizing for having groped her during their last shoot. "Sure, Eric. Don't even worry about it. I know what I need to do with this scene."

"Great." He gave her one of the devastating smiles that had made him a Hollywood icon, and Ivy admitted privately that she wasn't completely immune to the man's charm. He didn't appeal to her personally—her tastes ran more to the dark, dangerous type—but she could appreciate that he was a gorgeous man who had an ability to make a woman feel special just by the expression in his eyes.

"Okay, folks, let's do a walk-through. Where are Helena and Garrett?"

Finn turned from his consultation with the associate directors and scanned the set until he found Ivy and Eric. Ducking beneath Eric's arm, she stepped forward. "We're here."

Under the lights, she was aware of Eric at her elbow. Finn gave each of them a critical appraisal. "Okay, let's have some of the bruising around Stokes's left eye modified. I don't recall it being so vivid when he's first brought into the church."

Almost immediately, Denise and another makeup artist appeared with their tackle boxes of cosmetics and went to work on Eric's face. When they were through, Finn studied their handiwork and then grunted his approval. He gestured for Ivy to approach.

"Let's do a quick run-through. Ivy, you stand here and, Eric, you're already on the bed."

For the next forty minutes, Ivy was told exactly where to stand and where to move. She was grateful for the rehearsal; it gave her the time she needed to slowly bury her disquieting thoughts about Garrett and begin to absorb the make-believe world Finn had created. She tried not to think about the fact that Garrett hadn't shown up on the set for the shoot. It didn't mean anything. In all likelihood his expertise had been needed elsewhere, such as setting up the pyrotechnics for the explosive confrontation between the Special Forces soldiers and the Escudero cartel. Or he could be coordinating with the army for the Blackhawk helicopters scheduled to fly in next week for the final rescue scene. Whatever the reason, he obviously had more important things to do than watch her perform this scene. It was no big deal.

She concentrated on Finn's directions. Every time she stopped, someone would place a small piece of tape on the floor to mark the spot. She was aware of the camera following her slowly.

They rehearsed the scene once. Twice.

"Okay, let's go for a take," Finn called.

Ivy nodded and assumed her position for the opening of the scene. Finn checked the camera angle himself, then stepped onto the set to assess the lighting, before he stopped directly in front of Ivy, putting his hands on her shoulders.

"I was little rough on you the last time we tried to do this scene. You've already made love with Garrett—" He stopped abruptly as he realized what he'd said. "I mean, you've already made love to Garrett *in the film.* You've been together for the past three days, and the audience knows you're falling in love with him."

Ivy nodded, but scarcely heard Finn as he continued to speak to her. His words reverberated through her. "You've already made love with Garrett." *She was falling in love with him.* It was no less than the truth. She was falling in love with Garrett Stokes.

She clearly recalled how she'd felt on the set of those other films when she'd become involved with her leading men and had believed herself to be in love with *them*. At the time, she'd been convinced of it, but she hadn't felt then as she did now—disjointed. Fragmented. As though she was waiting; anticipating something and dreading it at the same time.

Shaking herself out of her reverie, she forced herself to listen to what Finn was saying, as he continued to give her tips.

"Remember," he said, as if he hadn't noticed her brief mental absence, "you don't know if your attempts to have him rescued will be successful. If he's rescued, he returns to the States. If that fails, he's a dead man. Either way, chances are good that you won't see each other again, so this is it—the only opportunity you'll have to show him what he's come to mean to you. Got it?"

Ivy nodded. He had no idea of the impact his words had on her. After the past two days with Garrett, there was a distinct possibility that this could very well be the end of their short-lived relationship. He'd said he wanted the full three days that she'd initially asked for, but the reality was that they might not have another opportunity to be together, even if she was inclined to believe he might still be interested.

Standing on the set, she mentally prepared herself for the fact that the cameras would be rolling in less than a minute and she had to act sexy while ten or more electricians and other crew members stood around munching on sandwiches as they watched her. But she realized that she didn't need to hide her distress at the thought that she and Garrett might be through, that what they'd shared might have been nothing more than a fling. Instead, she would channel all that emotion and uncertainty into her character. She took a deep breath.

Finn strode over to an empty chair beside the cameras and nodded to the man standing next to him, an assistant director named Franz Keller. Ivy was more than a little intimidated by the man, as he'd been hired by the producer to monitor the production company's investment. He kept order on the set and ensured the filming stayed on schedule. If he thought Ivy was a risk to the production, he'd be the one to contact the producer and have her replaced. If Ivy had to prove anything to anyone, it was to him.

"Quiet on the set!" Franz shouted.

"Take a medium shot," the cinematographer directed the cameraman.

"Roll it," said Franz.

"Rolling."

"Speed," called another assistant director. "Thirty-six, take nineteen."

A female assistant darted onto the set, held a slate in front of Ivy's face and flapped it shut.

"Action!" commanded Finn.

The next hour passed in a blur for Ivy as the film crew, lights and microphones disappeared and she became Helena. The scene involved her changing the dressing on Eric's leg, while she struggled to maintain her composure, knowing their time together was limited. The scene ended with Eric grasping her arms and pulling her across his prone body to stare deeply into her eyes, telling her without words what the audience would already have guessed—he loved her.

"Cut! Print it."

Finn's words snapped Ivy out of her dreamlike state. She pushed herself away from Eric and stood by the side of the bed for a moment, scarcely able to believe they wouldn't have to redo the scene. She knew from experience how rare it was to capture a scene on the first take.

Finn strode onto the set, and although he didn't smile, Ivy could see the approval in his eyes. "Good job. Great chemistry. Okay, let's go right into the next scene, where you make love. It's less than a minute of actual film time, so make it count. Ivy, go see makeup and get rid of the clothes." He turned to the rest of the film crew. "We resume shooting in fifteen minutes, folks."

They dispersed rapidly, having learned through experience to use their breaks when they had a chance. Ivy made her way to her dressing room, a small partitioned area at the rear of the converted warehouse. Based on how many times they'd had to shoot the love scene the last time, the crew obviously thought it might be a while before they had another break. She knew differently.

In her dressing room, she quickly shed the blouse and khaki pants, then donned the beige thong. Carla swiftly mussed her hair and smudged some color on her lips and cheekbones, making it appear as though she'd been thoroughly kissed.

"Here," she said, holding out a glass of juice with a straw sticking out the top. "Have something to drink now, while you have the chance."

"Thanks. Do you have any mints?" Ivy waggled her eyebrows at the other woman. "Big kiss scene coming up."

Carla grinned as she dropped several mints into Ivy's palm. "How many takes are you going for this time?"

Ivy popped the mints into her mouth and gave the other woman a tolerant look. "Hopefully, just one."

"Well, I wouldn't blame you if you went for twenty.

Eric Terrell is so hot I'd want to kiss him for hours." She sighed dramatically. "Some women have all the luck. Speaking of which…" She raised an eyebrow at Ivy. "Anything you want to share with me?"

Ivy frowned. "Like what?"

"Like the rumors I heard that you and Mr. Military Badass were caught making out in the hallway the other night—that's what."

Heat flooded Ivy's face. "Oh, that." She shrugged in what she hoped was a careless manner. "I ran into him at the pool and he walked me back to my room. We exchanged a kiss. No big deal."

Carla gave her a knowing look. "Yeah, right." She caught Ivy's chin in her hand and tipped her face up to the light, presumably to check her makeup, but there was no mistaking the genuine concern in her eyes. "Just be careful."

Twisting her face from Carla's hand, Ivy stared at her. "What do you mean?"

Carla shifted her attention to putting the array of cosmetics back in order. Her red curls bounced as she shook her head. "I'm just saying that sometimes staying on location, especially in a gorgeous place like this, has a way of distorting reality, you know? Makes you think you can live this kind of lifestyle forever." She shook her head. "But eventually, we all have to return to our real lives and sometimes that lifestyle just can't come with us."

Ivy stood, tightening the sash on her robe. She shot Carla a tolerant smile. "Thanks, but I've been doing this for a while, so you don't have to worry about me. I do know the difference between reality and make-believe."

Carla backed down. "If you say so."

An assistant stuck her head into the dressing room. "Five minutes," she announced, holding up her fingers.

Ivy nodded. "Thanks." She faced Carla. "Do I look okay?"

"Trust me, sweetie, you look stunning."

Ivy drew in a deep breath. "Okay, then. Wish me luck!"

"Yeah, right," grumbled the other woman, "like you don't already have more than your share of it. But, sure, break a leg."

As Ivy made her way back to the set, she tried not to think about whom she'd be kissing. It wouldn't be Eric Terrell, she told herself. It would be Garrett. She'd close her eyes and pretend it was Garrett. She knew firsthand what it was like to be in his arms, and she owed it to Finn to reveal just how amazing and beautiful the experience had been.

When she arrived on the set, she scanned the assembled crew swiftly, but Garrett still wasn't there. Part of her was relieved. The mere thought of him watching her make love to another man, while pretending it was *him,* made her insides turn to Jell-O. She wouldn't be able to do it when he was present.

Finn marched over to her, rapidly assessing her makeup. "Helena, good job on the last take. Now I want you to crank up the heat once you're in bed with Garrett, okay? I want this footage to leave scorch marks on the film, got it?"

Ivy nodded. "Got it."

Eric was already in position on the narrow bed. Tamping down her feelings of modesty, Ivy slid out of the robe and handed it to an assistant, before slipping beneath the covers next to Eric. His skin was warm, and he smelled faintly of licorice.

She lay back on the pillows and looked into his blue eyes, surprised to find him watching her. "What?"

He gave a small shake of his head. "I don't know. You seem different today. More relaxed, like you might not actually hate doing this."

Ivy couldn't help smiling. "Is that what you think? Well, let's just say I took Finn's recommendation and found my inspiration. Besides, half the women in the world would love to be me right now, so why not make the most of it?"

Eric let out a bark of surprised laughter. "Okay. Right. Well, let's show them how it's done."

He leaned in toward her, and Ivy forestalled him with a hand on his chest. "Within the parameters of the script, big guy."

He gave her a dramatically crestfallen expression. "If you insist."

"Oh, I do."

"Quiet on the set!" shouted Franz.

"Here we go," Eric murmured.

Ivy closed her eyes, conjuring up an image of a chiseled face with light-hazel eyes and slashing black eyebrows, knowing this might be the most difficult performance of her life.

"Cut!"

Ivy opened her eyes to find Eric Terrell staring down at her with something like astonishment in his eyes. She was still pressed against him, her arms wound around his neck. He braced himself on his elbows over her, and twin patches of color rode high on his cheekbones. His breathing was uneven.

"Holy shit," he finally croaked.

They'd done it. They'd managed to film the love scene in just two takes. Ivy couldn't quite believe it. Withdrawing her arms from where they were wound around Eric's neck, she nudged him and he complied by flopping back on the bed beside her.

Ivy pulled the sheet tighter around her body and glanced over at the crew, but the lights blinded her so that she couldn't see beyond the edge of the set itself. She was acutely conscious, though, of the overwhelming silence that greeted Finn's command to cut.

"Was that okay?" she at last was able to ask, shielding her eyes against the overhead glare.

"Print it," Finn boomed with a chortle.

Somebody off set began to clap. Another person joined in, and within seconds, Ivy and Eric were treated to a round of applause from the crew and cast members.

Finn stepped onto the set and approached the bed, carrying Ivy's robe in his hands. This time, there was no denying the wide grin that split his features.

"Well done," he said, handing her the garment. "That last take was—well, it was unbelievable. In a good way. So good, in fact, that it seemed like an intrusion to yell *'Cut.'*"

Ivy blushed. She had *really* gotten into character, convincing both her mind and body that Garrett was the one kissing her, stroking her. Garrett was the one whispering impassioned endearments against her skin. She had to give Finn credit, too. He'd remained almost entirely silent during the shoot, refraining from yelling instructions about how to move or where they should put their hands, instead letting them act out the scene on instinct.

It had worked.

Even now, her body thrummed with sexual need and frustration, as she'd responded with abandon to Eric's—*Garrett's*—touch.

"That was all I had scheduled for you today," Finn

said. "I didn't think you'd nail the scene so quickly." He grinned again, shaking his head in amazement. "I haven't seen chemistry like this since Russell Crowe and Meg Ryan made *Proof of Life*."

"Yeah, and look how that turned out," muttered Eric. "Their love scenes landed on the cutting-room floor because they were too realistic."

Finn laughed. "Believe me, yours are realistic. But we'll do some tasteful editing so the audience doesn't feel like they're sharing your breathing space." He looked directly at Ivy. "Trust me when I say this love scene will make you an overnight sensation."

Behind him, the lighting crew began shutting down the equipment, and when the overhead lights finally blinked off, Ivy could see beyond the perimeter of the set to the people who worked behind the scenes.

She caught her breath.

Was that Garrett standing with the film crew? With her eyes still adjusting to the abrupt change in light, it was difficult to tell for sure, but she thought she'd recognize that stance anywhere. Right now, he leaned against a door frame, arms crossed over his chest, and unless she was mistaken, he was gazing at her.

"Excuse me, please," she murmured to Eric and Finn, and got up, belting her robe securely as she began walking toward Garrett. He was mostly in the shadows, but she'd know those shoulders and lean hips anywhere. He didn't move as she approached, and not until she stood in front of him did she see the expression in his eyes.

She shivered.

A muscle flexed in his lean jaw and his eyes held a ravenous gleam. Had he seen the entire shoot? How did he feel about watching her get hot and heavy with Eric Terrell?

"How long have you been here?"

"Long enough," he growled. "Get dressed and let's go."

"Where?" She couldn't suppress the thrum of anticipation his words caused.

"Anywhere."

"Okay." She sensed his impatience. "I'll just be a few minutes."

"I'll wait."

But as Ivy hurried to the dressing room, she was aware that her heart was beating faster and her legs felt a little wobbly. She thought she understood now why the film was called *Eye of the Hunter*—the look in Garrett's eyes had been completely predatory.

12

GARRETT WATCHED IVY walk away, her bare feet padding on the ancient wooden floors of the warehouse-turned-film-set. She stopped briefly when Franz Keller, the assistant director, intercepted her to hand her a slip of paper. Her call sheet for the following day, Garrett guessed. She and Franz spoke briefly, then Franz glanced in his direction with a knowing expression. He said something to Ivy that made her stiffen, before she crumpled the paper in her hand and stalked away.

Garrett scowled at the other man. From the smugness on Keller's face, Garrett had a good idea of what the man had said. He wanted to follow her into the dressing room and demand she tell him Franz's words. Then he'd take care of it.

He groaned and raked a hand through his hair, knowing he had to get a grip on himself. Anyone who looked at him right now would see the truth about his feelings for Ivy, and he'd made a promise to himself that he wouldn't put her in this position. If she wanted to go public about the two of them, that was fine with him. But if she wanted to keep their affair secret, he wouldn't do anything to compromise that.

He'd caught the pleasure in her eyes when she'd first spotted him, then the alarm that had flared in their chocolate depths when he'd told her to get dressed. But she'd agreed to go with him. That was the important thing.

The shoot had gone so well he'd needed all his self-restraint not to stride onto the set and drag Ivy out of the bed and out of Terrell's arms. He still couldn't believe the difference between her first attempt at that scene and what he'd just witnessed. He'd felt like a voyeur. Watching them, he found it hard to accept that they weren't actually banging for the camera beneath the concealing sheet.

He told himself they'd only been acting, but his gut twisted with jealousy. *Had* they just been acting, or had Ivy finally succumbed to the actor's allure? He almost couldn't blame her if she had. If the tabloids were to be credited, Terrell was the embodiment of just about every female fantasy in America. Then there was Ivy's own history of falling for her leading men. Garrett already knew she had a soft heart and a tendency to mistake on-screen love for the real thing. Yet he also knew any relationship with Terrell would only end in disaster. The guy was incapable of fidelity. Just the thought of Terrell taking advantage of Ivy in that way made his hands curl into fists.

He absolutely wanted Ivy to succeed; he wanted her to blow Finn away with the quality of her acting skills. He just hadn't counted on his own reaction to the sight of Ivy plastered against Terrell.

Outwardly, he'd remained impassive. Inwardly, he'd felt rabid. He'd observed the scene from a distance, staying just out of her line of vision. He hadn't wanted to distract her, but man, oh, man, it had been tough to stay where he was and not interfere with the shoot.

But when the filming had ended and Ivy had walked toward him wearing no more than a dressing robe, her lips still swollen from Terrell's kisses, he'd had a primitive and nearly overwhelming urge to toss her over his shoulder and carry her off somewhere private.

He wanted to possess her, take her fiercely and endlessly. Leave her in absolutely no doubt about whose arms she belonged in. Only with supreme effort had he kept his hands shoved firmly in his pockets and relaxed indifference in his posture as he'd watched her walk toward the dressing rooms.

When she returned less than ten minutes later, she had on the same sundress she'd worn the first night she'd come out to his cabin. She carried an oversize tote over one shoulder and her face still bore the remnants of makeup from her shoot. But as she drew closer, he saw that the tender skin of her neck and jaw was red and abraded from whisker burn. Terrell's whiskers.

The sight was enough to snap the vestiges of his self-control. Not caring who saw them or what they might think, he caught Ivy's arm and propelled her toward the door.

"Whoa, where's the fire?" she asked, laughing.

They were outside now, and without answering, Garrett pushed her up against the wall, thrusting his fingers into the silken warmth of her hair as he devoured her with his eyes.

She stared up at him, her eyes questioning, before her gaze fell to his mouth. As if unable to help herself, she let out a soft sigh and her lips parted, as if anticipating his kiss. But he didn't kiss her.

Not yet.

"Jesus, Ivy," he muttered, fastening his attention on her mouth as he smoothed a thumb over her lower lip. "I saw Terrell kissing you and I wanted to kill the son of a bitch."

Her eyes widened momentarily at his words. "Trust me when I say that it was all an act. In fact," she confessed, "I was thinking of you when we did that scene. I just closed my eyes and pretended I was in your arms—"

"It was a little too realistic for me," Garrett growled. "Finn might have to change the film rating given how realistic that last scene was."

To his amazement, she smiled. "Why does that sound like a good thing?"

Garrett groaned. "Good for you, maybe, but sheer hell for me. That *was* the last shoot where you have to get naked with Terrell, right?"

Her smile deepened. "This is your story. You tell me."

IVY WATCHED, MESMERIZED, as Garrett's eyes darkened. He made a low sound of frustration and hauled her in against his body, surrounding her with his warmth, hardness and scent, before covering her mouth with his own.

The kiss was primal, designed to possess and dominate. Ivy welcomed it, even encouraged it by winding her arms around his neck and meeting the fierceness with unabashed enthusiasm. She didn't deny that the love scene with Eric had left her aroused, but it couldn't compare with what this man did to her with his touch. Need, hot and greedy, spiraled through her. Beneath the thin fabric of the sundress, her breasts tightened and a familiar ache blossomed between her thighs. She was vaguely aware she and Garrett were outside, where anyone might view them, but she didn't care.

She still couldn't believe he was here. Despite the fact that not even a full day had passed since she'd last been with him, she'd missed him. She'd all but given up on seeing him on the set. Of seeing him again at all. Sure, he'd said he wanted the full three days they'd agreed to, but Ivy had figured that was just talk.

She'd never been so glad to be wrong.

Knowing that he'd watched her with Eric Terrell caused a naughty thrill to course through her. What had he thought of her performance? Had it turned him on? She'd tried so hard to capture the essence of what she'd shared with Garrett—the urgency and the tenderness and the overwhelming desire. Had she succeeded?

Voices drifted toward them from just inside the warehouse, and Ivy realized somebody was approaching. In another second, she and Garrett would be discovered. She had to put some distance between them.

She dragged her mouth from his, her breathing uneven. "We can't do this…not here."

Garrett lifted his head. He appeared dazed, as if he'd forgotten where they were.

"Right," he muttered. "C'mon."

Before she could protest, he was leading her along the path from the warehouse to an adjacent field that doubled as a parking lot. Dusk had fallen as they made their way to the back of the field. No one else was around, and the air was fragrant with the scent of hibiscus. A dozen or so vehicles were parked haphazardly on the grass, including the Jeep that Garrett had driven that first day she'd arrived in Pancho Viejo.

He opened the door to the vehicle, but when she hitched her skirt up to climb in, he halted her.

"Ivy."

She looked up and was trapped in the intensity of his gaze. Instead of handing her up into the passenger seat, he pressed her against the side of the Jeep, imprisoning her with his own body. "I'm sorry, babe," he growled, "but I can't wait another second."

He encircled her face with his large palms and slanted his lips across hers in a kiss that rocked her all the way down to her toes. She sighed into his mouth and arched against him, all thoughts of maintaining any distance from him completely gone. If she had her way, there would be absolutely nothing between them. Desire curled through her as he deepened the kiss, tangling his tongue with hers and feasting on her lips.

Oh, God. If he didn't stop, she was going to haul him into the Jeep and beg him to make love to her right then and there. She dragged her mouth from his, breathless.

"Please," she panted.

He cupped her face and his fingers massaged the tender skin behind her ears. His eyes glowed as he regarded her. "Please...what?" His voice was husky.

Ivy swallowed. "Please don't, because if not, I won't be responsible for my actions."

His smile broadened, and he dropped his forehead to hers. "Sounds tempting. I think I have a blanket or two in the back, and I know a little place about two minutes from here where the stargazing is phenomenal." His voice was languid and full of promise.

Ivy's body responded instantly, liquid heat pooling in her center. Her breasts ached where they were pressed against his chest. She wondered briefly if becoming addicted to someone's touch was possible. She didn't want to wait. She wanted him, and she wanted him now.

"Let's just drive," she whispered, pulling his head down, "and see where we end up." Her eyes fluttered closed, and then his tongue was in her mouth again as he flattened her against the side of the Jeep and devoured her.

He tore his mouth from hers. "Jesus. Let's get out of here before I do something lewd in a public place."

He helped her into the cab and popped a cassette into the stereo. Soft music filled the interior of the Jeep as he maneuvered the vehicle out of the field and onto the rutted dirt road that led back to the hacienda. He glanced over at her. "We'll be at the hacienda in less than ten minutes."

It was all Ivy could do not to groan her frustration.

His hand settled on her leg, warm and sure, and then he was pushing back the hem of her sundress and skating his palm over the smooth skin of her bare thigh. Ivy caught her breath, and, when he would have explored further, stopped him with her hand on his. She stared at him, half hopeful and half uncertain in the dim light.

"Trust me." The glance he gave her was at once so heated and tender that she loosed her grip on him, although she kept her fingers over his. "Now, sit back and pull your skirt up. That's it."

"I don't recall this being in the script," she said, her voice husky, even as she obeyed him.

"Screw the script," he declared, his eyes hot as they locked onto her. "We're writing our own scenes from here on."

Ivy could scarcely believe she was doing as he asked, hiking her skirt up over hips so that her entire lower half was exposed but for the scrap of lace that was her panties. She was pulsing with need. Just looking at Garrett as he watched her was enough for her to become slick with desire. His gaze on her was as palpable as a caress.

He drew in a hissing breath as his eyes traveled down the length of her, and his hand stroked upward from her knee to the apex of her thighs.

"Open for me," he commanded quietly.

"Garrett…"

"Please, sweetheart. I have to touch you."

His voice was gruff with need, and with a groan that was half mortification, half anticipation, Ivy let her thighs fall apart. And then there was no more room for coherent thought as he cupped her through the damp material of her panties. She gasped and her hips arched against his palm. When he pushed the scrap of fabric aside and caressed her intimately, she mewled in pleasure.

"That's it," he murmured approvingly, and slid a finger into her slick heat.

Ivy's head fell back against the seat as his hand worked its magic, pushing her and teasing her. She was only vaguely aware of the thick forest and dense overhead canopy flying past the windows of the Jeep. She knew she should tell him to slow down, but she wanted him to go faster; didn't want to wait a second longer than she had to, to feel him inside her. His fingers were sliding over her flesh, and she was close to flying apart. With the last vestiges of rational thought, she gripped his wrist and forced him to halt.

"Please," she gasped, "I don't want to…until you can come with me."

GARRETT, ALREADY INTENSELY aroused, felt himself swell even more at her words. He tore his attention from the road and stared at her for the briefest of seconds, taking in her flushed features and glazed eyes. The Jeep surged as he leaned even harder on the accelerator, and then, thank God, the turnoff that led to the hacienda appeared. He didn't pull into the circular drive that led to the entrance, however. He veered off the main drive and onto a deeply rutted dirt path. He skirted the property and they bounced through a heavily forested section of jungle before the trees cleared and the workers' cabins came into view.

The Jeep barely skidded to a full stop behind his own *casita* before he leaped out. He didn't even give Ivy time to adjust her clothing before he tore open her door and hauled her into his arms. With a gasp, she flung her arms around his shoulders and clung for dear life. He kicked the door of the truck closed and carried her into the cabin.

Inside, he pushed her up against the wall, letting her legs slide to the floor. Her eyes were wide as she stared up him, her lips slightly parted. With a groan, he bent his head and claimed her lips. He thrust his hands into the mass of her hair, reveling in the silken texture of the tight curls and how they clung to his fingers.

Jesus, she felt so good in his arms. She still hung on to him; only now her fingers were stroking the back of his neck. He was pressed against her from shoulder to knee; knew she could feel his arousal against her belly. He couldn't remember the last time he had been this turned on. Well, okay, that wasn't true. Yesterday probably ran a close tie. Christ, he couldn't get enough of her. She felt so good beneath his hands.

With a rough sound of need, he grasped her buttocks, raising her and pressing himself into the soft cradle of her hips. To his delight, she responded by pushing her hands beneath his shirt and smoothing her palms over his skin, touching every part of him she could get to. He groaned at the sensation of her cool fingers against his heated flesh.

"Garrett," she whispered against his lips, "please…"

"This is real," he muttered against her lips, wanting to make sure she understood. "The other stuff—the scene with Terrell—that was all just make-believe. This is real. Tell me you know this is real."

"This is real," she repeated raggedly. "I know the difference."

"Do you?"

"Yes," she gasped. "Please..."

He lifted her higher against the wall, then fumbled beneath her silk-clad bottom to awkwardly work the snap on his jeans. All he could think about was being inside her, being part of her. She'd occupied his mind every moment since he'd left her at the hacienda the night before. He hadn't slept. He hadn't given a thought to the film, or his own responsibilities to it. He'd been consumed with thoughts of Ivy.

Of being with her again.

He'd hated watching her with Eric Terrell. Not only because he suspected the other man was enjoying the scene way too much, but because he already considered Ivy his own.

He slanted his mouth hard across hers, wanting to possess her completely. With one hand beneath her, he worked his wallet free from his back pocket with his other hand, then flipped it open and located the condom he'd put there just that morning. Dropping the wallet onto the floor, he tore the small packet open with his teeth, his eyes never leaving Ivy's. One hand still supporting her bottom, he freed himself, pushed his briefs and pants down and out of the way, then rolled the sheath over his erection.

His bad leg protested the strain of supporting Ivy, but he scarcely noticed. She moaned as he pressed, hard and hot, against the most intimate part of her. He had no problem sliding a hand between their straining bodies and tearing aside the minuscule scrap of lace that covered her, and then, sweet, blessed Mary, he was pushing himself into her welcoming moistness.

She gasped in pleasure and raised her legs higher, wrapping them around his hips even as she met the thrusts of his tongue against hers with equal fervor. God, she felt incredible, all slick heat and pulsating tightness. He grasped her silken buttocks in his hands and thrust himself into her, knowing he wasn't being gentle, but beyond the point where he could restrain himself.

She rode him just as powerfully, gripping his hips with her thighs and using them to lever herself up and down on his shaft. Her fingers speared through his hair and she was moaning into his mouth, making small sounds of pleasure and rising need.

He dragged his mouth from hers and used one hand to swiftly undo the little buttons at the top of her dress, all the while maintaining the aerobic pace she was setting.

"I want to see you," he growled, and pushed the fabric aside until her breasts sprang free. She wasn't wearing a bra and her nipples were tightly erect, straining toward him. With a groan, he bent his head and drew one into his mouth, suckling her hard. She cried out and arched her back, and he felt her tightening around him, squeezing him until, with a harsh cry, he climaxed in a surge of exquisite pleasure. They stood locked together for a full minute, until his legs began to tremble with fatigue. Through a haze of mindless bliss, he turned and shuffled the few steps to the bed, where his bad leg finally gave out, tumbling Ivy and him onto the mattress.

Ivy still straddled his hips, and her face was pressed against his neck. Her breathing was uneven, and his sounded harsh in the silence of the little cabin. She laughed and wrapped her arms around him, pressing closer.

"I have never done anything so—so—*wild* in my entire life," she said breathlessly. "My God, it's not even fully dark outside."

"So?"

She pushed her hair back from where it obscured her face and gave him a look of astonishment. "So...I let you touch me *there*. In the Jeep. While we were driving! Anyone could have seen us."

"The doors were on and the top was up," Garrett reassured her, struggling to catch his breath. "Even if anyone was looking—which they weren't—they couldn't see anything. Which reminds me...what did Franz say to you on the set?"

"What?"

"Franz Keller said something to you when he handed you the call sheet for tomorrow. What was it?"

She was quiet for a moment, before she withdrew her limbs from where they were entwined around him and slowly pushed her skirt back down over her legs. "Nothing. He's just a thoughtless jerk."

But Garrett knew from the subdued tone of her voice that it wasn't something good. He stood up, disposed of the condom and pulled his jeans up over his hips. "Fine. If you don't tell me, then I'll ask him."

"No. Wait." Ivy sat up and grabbed his wrist. "I'll tell you. Only, please don't say anything to him. He didn't mean anything by it. He was just looking out for the project, and that's his job, right?"

"What did he say?"

She regarded him for a long minute, and Garrett could see the distress in her eyes before she chewed her lower lip and gazed down at her hands. "He said he knew my M.O. is to sleep with my leading man, and he doesn't really mind as long as it doesn't interfere with his production schedule."

"Son of a bitch." Garrett didn't care who the little bastard worked for; he was going to pay him an unpleasant visit. He yanked the zipper up on his jeans. "Wait here. This won't take long."

Ivy leaped to her feet. "What are you going to do?"

Garrett hesitated. Her eyes were wide and filled with dread, and he realized that he'd only make things worse for her by interfering. Just like that, the fight went out of him. "Come here." He drew her close.

"I don't think he actually meant to insult me when he said it," she insisted, her voice muffled against his chest. "It's just what people expect from me." She gave a laugh of self-disgust. "I haven't let them down."

Garrett pulled back and gazed into Ivy's eyes. "Is that what you think?"

She looked at him silently.

"Jesus, Ivy." He set her at arm's length. "How many movies have you made?"

She shrugged. "Ten."

"And how many of those have resulted in a relationship with a costar?"

Her eyes begged him not to continue, even as she tried to edge away from him, but he refused to release her.

"How many, Ivy?"

She made a sound of frustration and resignation. "Three, okay? I was involved with three of my costars."

"Three," he breathed, "over the course of how many years? Four? Five?"

As if he didn't already know.

"Something like that."

Garrett tipped his head to look into her face. "That hardly qualifies you as 'Firecrotch of the Year.'"

Her eyes widened and then she grinned. "Where did you hear that term?"

"It doesn't matter," he said, refusing to be sidetracked. "The important thing to remember is that you're human, and you're subject to the same foibles as the rest of us." He let his gaze drift over her features. "There are worse things in life than falling in love."

"But that's just it," she protested, searching his eyes. "I only thought I was in love. I let myself be influenced by the characters we were portraying, and by the surroundings." She gestured helplessly. "What I felt wasn't love. Just a cheap Hollywood imitation of it."

She sounded so miserable that Garrett couldn't help but hug her. "Listen to me. We all make mistakes. If you knew half the things I've done…" His voice trailed off. Even if he wanted to tell her about his military experiences, he couldn't. "Let's just say I've done shit because at the time it was the right thing to do. But if there's one thing I've learned, it's that you can't spend your life regretting your past or you'll miss out on your future." He put a finger beneath her chin and raised her face, studying her. "Got it?"

She wrapped her fingers around his hand and a ghost of a smile touched her lips. "You don't think less of me for those past relationships?"

"I'd be lying if I said they didn't bother me," he finally acknowledged, his voice rough. "The fact is, I'm jealous as hell of the men you've been with, because I know a bit of you will always belong to them."

Ivy disentangled her fingers from his and moved away from him, scrubbing her hands over her face. "This is crazy," she muttered. "I've only known you a short time. How can I feel this way about you?"

Garrett stilled. "How do you feel, Ivy?"

She turned toward him, and her eyes shimmered. She shrugged helplessly and her voice was little more than a whisper.

"Like I'm falling in love with you."

13

SILENCE FILLED THE SMALL cabin.

Ivy stared at Garrett, hardly daring to breathe. She still couldn't believe she'd uttered the words, but he had that effect on her. She felt as though she'd known him for so much longer than the short time they'd been in Mexico. It was as if they were connected on a level she couldn't even begin to comprehend. She'd felt an affinity with him from the first day they'd met, and it had only grown stronger during the time they'd been together.

Now, as she saw him stand so still, so stunned, her chest constricted. She'd just made a huge mistake.

Again.

Mortification, hot and swift, flooded her veins, followed by a chilling sense of loss. How could she have been so stupid? If she'd just kept her mouth shut...if she hadn't blurted out her feelings...

She needed to get out of there before she did something she'd really regret, like start to cry.

"I—I'm sorry," she muttered. "I shouldn't have said that. It's too soon."

Before he could protest, she bolted for the door. Her bare foot kicked his wallet where it still lay, and she automatically bent to retrieve it.

"Ivy, wait—"

"Here," she said, thrusting it blindly at him.

As she did so, the contents slid out and Ivy watched helplessly as credit cards, money, several receipts and a folded photograph fluttered to the floor.

The event galvanized Garrett into action. He lunged at the same instant Ivy hunched down to scoop up the photo.

"I'll have that," he said, and grabbed for her hands.

But Ivy had already seen what he was attempting so desperately to retrieve from her. She couldn't prevent a small gasp of astonishment as she snatched the photograph away from him and held it just out of reach, while letting him keep the other items. She was only vaguely aware of him sitting down heavily on the floor, his shoulders sagging.

"Where did you get this?" She unfolded the snapshot, smoothing her fingers over the dog-eared corners and deep creases. "How could you have this?"

It was the photograph she'd taken with her to Walter Reed Army Medical Center two years ago when she'd visited her brother.

She'd also brought flowers and magazines, hoping to cheer him up, not understanding that he wasn't going to recover. In the end, she'd left just the photograph, placing it gently on the blanket that covered him. He'd snapped the picture of her the summer before his last deployment, and had been ridiculously pleased with the results.

"I'd carry it with me," he'd joked, "but all the guys would hound me for your address. I'd never have any peace."

Seeing the photo again brought forth all her suppressed memories, and hot tears blurred her vision. She turned to look at Garrett. His arms rested on his bent knees and one hand swiped wearily at his face.

"Where did you get this?" Her voice was little more than a whisper.

He made a helpless gesture, and even through her tears she could see the resignation and defeat on his chiseled features. "I shared a room with your brother."

"What?" She still didn't understand.

"I was in the bed next to his at Walter Reed," he continued. "I'd just been airlifted out of Colombia and had undergone surgery on my leg." He raised his head to her, and Ivy noticed compassion in his eyes. "I was there when your brother died. I saw you leave the photo."

She frowned as she fought her tears, trying vainly to recall her brother's hospital room and the man who'd occupied the other bed. The memory was hazy—she'd kept it buried for so long—but it was there. She struggled to bring it to the surface, and when it finally came into focus, she eyed him in astonishment.

"It was you!"

"Yeah."

"That's why you seemed so familiar to me...I remember your eyes. You looked right at me."

"Yeah, I did."

"Oh, my God." Her breath emerged in a hard rush, and she felt weak. "You stole my photo."

Garrett pushed himself to his feet. "Now, wait just a minute. I did not *steal* it."

Ivy, too, rose to her feet. She held the photo out to him, unable to keep the accusatory tone from her voice. "Then tell me how you have this."

"It fell off your brother's bed and landed under mine. A couple of days later the cleaning guy found it and put it on my side table." He met her gaze without flinching. "I've kept it ever since."

"Why?"

He stepped toward her and his hands closed around hers.

"Why do you think?" His voice was low and fierce.

She shook her head, staring at him in bemusement. "I'm not sure, but I do know one thing—my being here to film *your* story is no coincidence. Is it?"

He didn't answer, but she heard his deep sigh. He didn't look at her. Wordlessly, he gathered up the items on the floor and took the photo from her, then replaced them in his wallet, turning it over in his hands before shoving the wallet into his back pocket. She could see he struggled to form a reply.

"What?" she asked. Her heart was pounding so hard she was sure he could hear it. "What is it? Why am I really here?" She gave a disbelieving laugh. "Why do I get the sense that my being cast in this role has nothing to do with my acting skills and everything to do with you?"

When he finally looked at her, Ivy couldn't deny the truth in his eyes. They were filled with so much regret and resignation that she wanted to cry out in denial.

"Ivy…"

"Oh, my God. It's true," she whispered, one hand at her throat. "That's it, isn't it? What did you do, Garrett? Refuse to let Finn make the movie unless they cast me?"

"Damn it, Ivy, would you slow down for just a minute and let me explain?"

Ivy flung her arms wide, too shocked and hurt to hear the growing impatience in his voice. "Explain what? That I wasn't hired on my own merit? That this was all a big setup, and I'm nothing more than an elaborate booty call?"

"You know that's not true." His voice was low and edged with an anger that Ivy couldn't miss but was just reckless enough to ignore.

"Then what is the truth, Garrett? Because I don't know anymore. What did you think—that since I have a history of sleeping with my costars, I'd be an easy lay for you?"

She didn't actually believe her own words, but she felt an irresistible urge to lash out at him. She knew she'd hit her target when he flinched, but he refused to back down.

He grasped her by the upper arms and gave her a little shake. "If the only thing I wanted was casual sex, I wouldn't have to come all the way to Mexico to get it," he growled. "I already told you. This is *real.* You want more truth?"

The expression on his face was so taut and his eyes so intense that Ivy's breath caught. She tried to look away, to break free, but found herself mesmerized.

"You're here because I haven't been able to stop thinking about you. Before he died, Devon asked me to watch over you. Trust me, it was no hardship. Since the day I saw you in that hospital, there's been nobody else." He gave a self-deprecating laugh. "Call me crazy—you wouldn't be the first. But trust me when I say that my feelings for you are real."

Ivy stared at him, wanting desperately to believe him. "But my being cast in this film…"

He closed his eyes briefly. "Finn is my brother-in-law."

"What?"

"He's married to my sister, Savannah. I stayed with them while I was recuperating. However, the idea to turn my combat experiences into a movie was strictly his."

Ivy pulled free from his grasp, struggling to digest

what he'd said. "Nevertheless, the decision to cast me in this role was yours. Not Finn's."

It wasn't a question; it was a statement. And she knew from his face that she was right. Her mind spun with the ugly implications. "Maybe I should be grateful to you for providing me with this opportunity," she said, rubbing her hands over the goose bumps on her bare arms. "Maybe you think you've fulfilled your promise to Devon by helping me out. But how can I feel good about something I didn't earn? Finn didn't offer me this role because he believes in me—"

"*I* believe in you." He took a step toward her, his eyes seeming to glow with an inner fire. "Doesn't that count for something? And let's face it. Finn would never have agreed to bring you on board if he didn't think you'd be perfect for the part. End of story. I may have steered him in your direction, but the final decision was his and his alone."

"I wish I could accept that. But at the moment, I'm not sure what to think." Ivy pressed her fingers against her temples. "It's like this whole thing was an act."

"You said you were falling in love with me," Garrett told her, his voice insistent. "That wasn't an act. And these past two days together…they weren't an act either. You can't look at me and tell me you think I was just using you."

Ivy blinked. He was right. None of it had been an act. She'd never felt as real as she had in Garrett's arms. Even now, the look in his eyes threatened to undo her. His admission that he'd been attracted to her since the day he'd first seen her turned her insides to complete mush. She knew enough about the entertainment industry to understand that getting her onto this movie set couldn't have been easy. That in itself was a strong statement about his feelings for her. And it was just like Devon to appoint a guardian to watch over her after he died. Garrett would have had a hard time refusing him. It was almost enough to make her forgive Garrett.

Almost.

But then she remembered how Eric Terrell had treated her when she'd first arrived, as though she wasn't worthy to work alongside him. She thought of Finn MacDougall, one of the greatest directors in Hollywood, casting her—a virtual unknown—in the lead female role. She recalled again what he'd said to her during that first awful attempt to shoot the love scene: *I brought you onto this project with some reservations, but you came so highly recommended that I decided to offer you a chance.*

She didn't have to guess who had recommended her so highly. It was too humiliating even to contemplate.

"I did say I was falling in love with you," she began slowly, "but the truth is, the guy I was falling in love with turned out to be just like all the other guys I fell for—a fraud."

Garrett went still and a muscle flexed in his jaw. "That's bullshit and you know it."

Ivy swiped a hand across her eyes, feeling deflated and weary. "I don't know what to think anymore." She brushed past him without meeting his eyes, and paused with one hand on the screened door. "Look, I understand your intentions were good, and I appreciate everything you've done for me, but I don't think we should continue…whatever it is we've been doing here."

"I meant what I said." His voice was rough. "What we have together is real, Ivy."

"But that's just it, don't you see?" When she looked at him, his image wavered, and she realized she'd started to cry in earnest. "If you knew me—really knew me—then you'd know how important it is for me to do this on my own. My God, here I thought I was brought into this project because somebody had finally recognized and appreciated my talents as an actor. That's all I've ever wanted—to make it on my own merit. And you took that away from me."

"Ivy—"

She threw up a forestalling hand and gave him an imploring look. "No, don't say anything, please. I—I just have to go."

She left, walking swiftly out of the cabin and along the path that led to the hacienda before he could say something to make her change her mind and stay.

He didn't follow her.

As she made her way toward the hacienda, her mind turned over everything he'd told her. He'd shared a room with Devon. He'd watched her place the photo on Devon's chest. She'd had an uncanny sense of familiarity since the moment she'd first met Garrett on that rain-drenched roadside in Pancho Viejo, but she'd never have guessed who he was.

That one moment when their eyes had met hadn't been significant for her, but it had been for him. He'd kept her photo. He'd followed her career. He'd arranged for her to be cast in a role that any number of A-list actresses would have given their eyeteeth for. He'd said there hadn't been anyone else for him since he'd first laid eyes on her.

It was so clear to her now. *He loved her.*

She stopped at the entrance to the hacienda. She was an idiot to even think twice about why she'd been chosen for the part. The simple truth was that here was a man who thought enough of her to make her dreams come true. He'd said he believed in her. If she really loved him, that should be enough.

She realized it was.

Taking a deep breath, she wiped her cheeks and tried to compose herself before she walked—okay, ran—back down that path to his cottage and flung herself against his chest.

"Hey, sweetie, what're you doing out here? I saw you leave with Mr. Military Badass and I figured that by now, he'd be showing you his...tattoos."

Ivy turned to see Carla strolling toward her from the parking lot, where the small shuttle bus had just dropped off several members of the film crew. Ivy forced herself to smile, hoping the darkness concealed her reddened eyes.

"He doesn't have any."

"Are you sure? No heart tattoo with *Helena* scrawled across it?"

Ivy smiled uncertainly. "I'm sure. Besides, that relationship ended when he was airlifted out of Colombia. Despite what the script implies, they didn't actually see each other again after he was rescued."

Carla frowned. "Really."

"Really."

"Well, then he's in for quite a surprise."

An unaccountable dread gripped Ivy. "Why?"

"I just overheard Finn talking with the associate directors. It seems Helena Vanderveer is ill. She's leaving Colombia and returning to Amsterdam for treatment. But first she's stopping here to see Garrett. It appears she wants a reunion with her rescued soldier."

Ivy's heart stopped. She felt the color drain from her face. She knew Garrett loved her; she knew it with every fiber of her being. But the news that Helena would be here—in the flesh—caused her chest to constrict with fear.

What if he saw Helena and realized he was still in love with her? Maybe he'd decide to go to the Netherlands with her to support her through her illness, to be there for her the way Helena had been there for him.

Oh, God, could it get any worse? She tried desperately to recall what horrible things she'd said to Garrett in those emotionally charged moments before she'd fled his *casita*. Had she given him the impression they were through? She groaned silently as awful recollection flooded back. She'd called him a fraud. She'd denied that what they'd shared was real. She'd pushed him away from her, and now she had to face the possibility that she may have succeeded in pushing him right into another woman's arms.

She pressed her fingers against her eye sockets, only distantly aware of Carla watching her. She couldn't think straight. She felt sick to her stomach. If Garrett chose to go back to Helena, she'd have no one to blame but herself.

Smoothing her hands over her face, she looked at Carla. "When is she supposed to arrive?"

Carla's expression was apologetic. "Tomorrow."

14

Ivy perched on the edge of her bed and drew in a deep, calming breath. Morning sunlight slanted through the casement windows and the vibrant trill of a songbird filled the room. Despite a hot shower and a fresh sundress, courtesy of Carla, she felt exhausted and a little ill from lack of sleep.

With a sigh, she unfolded the crumpled piece of paper she held in her hand and smoothed it out on the bed. It was the call sheet that Franz Keller had handed to her the day before, and per the schedule, she had less than two hours before she had to be on the set, which meant she really should be heading over to hair and makeup.

Had it really been less than a day since her awful confrontation with Garrett? Since she'd learned that Helena Vanderveer was on her way to the movie location? An eternity seemed to have passed since Garrett had taken her up against the wall of his *casita*, making her lose control of herself.

Again.

She hadn't returned to his cabin. Hadn't trusted herself to behave with any level of dignity. She'd been too afraid she'd break down and beg him not to leave her. She'd been even more afraid he'd reject her. When she finally confronted him—and she had every intention of doing so—she wanted to be strong and in control. She just needed to summon the courage to see him. She understood why he'd done what he had, but at the same time, she had to make him realize how important it was that she succeed on her own.

She wondered if he'd come to the shoot. The cowardly part of her hoped he wouldn't be there to oversee filming of the scene, while the womanly part of her longed to make things right again between them.

She pushed herself to her feet and peered critically into the mirror. Her face was pale. Her eyes were puffy and red-rimmed from a sleepless night where she'd alternately wallowed in self-pity and railed against the poor timing of the Dutch missionary's reunion with Garrett. The one thing she hadn't done was sleep.

Fingering her hair into a semblance of order, she wondered if Helena had arrived yet. What did she look like? Had she and Garrett already had their happy reunion? Ivy imagined them in his cabin, their hands all over each other, before she determinedly pushed the images out of her head. She had no reason to believe Garrett would still be interested in the missionary, but the only way she would know for sure was to see him.

God, she needed to see him.

She grabbed her tote bag, flung it over one shoulder and opened the door. As she descended the curving staircase that led to the foyer, voices drifted up to her. She recognized Finn's distinctive baritone, and hurried the last few steps, hoping to speak with him in private before he left the hacienda. He maintained an aggressive personal schedule that often made catching him alone difficult.

He was sitting at a small table in the breakfast room adjacent to the lobby, drinking a cup of coffee and reading a newspaper. It was such a departure from his typical routine of grabbing a coffee and yogurt to go that Ivy hesitated for a moment, unsure if she should disturb him. Josephina was clearing away the remnants of his breakfast, along with two other place settings.

He glanced up as she approached.

"Ivy," he said, half rising to his feet. "Join me for a cup of coffee. I was hoping to talk to you before the shoot today. I don't know if you've heard, but we have a visitor I think you'll be interested in meeting."

She pulled out a chair and sat down. "Yes, I've heard," she said dully. "Helena Vanderveer."

His bushy eyebrows rose fractionally. "Oh. Well, that's great you know. Actually, you just missed her. We had breakfast together."

Ivy eyed the dirty dishes in Josephina's hands. Now she knew that one of them had been Helena's. Had the other one belonged to Garrett?

Ivy leaned forward. "Finn," she said, her voice low and earnest, "I need to ask you a question, and I want you to be completely honest with me."

Wariness crept over his face. "Sure. But if it's about yesterday's shoot, I meant what I said. It was sensational."

"Thanks." She looked down at her hands, clenched in her lap, then back at him. "I'm glad to hear you say that, because I heard…"

"Yes?" His expression was cautious. "What did you hear?"

"That you only brought me onto this project as a favor to Garrett Stokes, not because of my acting abilities," she blurted. There. She'd said it.

To her astonishment, Finn started to laugh. Then, seeing her face, he brought his napkin to his lips and coughed into it, instead. When he could, he set the linen down and looked at her tolerantly.

"Let me tell you one thing about myself, Ivy. I never, *ever* allow an actor to be cast in one of my films without my approval. I watch every audition, I look at every screen test and I review every past project. Furthermore—" he leaned toward her, his eyes growing hard "—I would never compromise my integrity or my project by casting somebody strictly as a favor to another person, even if they were the most talented actor in Hollywood. Got that?"

Ivy swallowed. "So you're saying it's not true. You brought me on board solely because of my own merit as an actor."

He arched an eyebrow, and a hint of a smile curved his lips. "Well, let's just say I was turned on to you by somebody who really loved your work and believed in your talent. And once I had a chance to see it for myself, I had to agree. So…yes. You were cast solely on the basis of your talent and your looks, and not because my brother-in-law has a hard-on for you." He lifted his coffee cup. "Is that clear enough for you?"

"Oh." Heat warmed her face.

"Mmm, *oh.* I was a little surprised to find you with him when I returned from Xalapa." He shrugged. "Not so much that he was with you, because he's made it pretty clear from day one that he's crazy about you. I just didn't think the feeling would be so mutual…so quickly."

He was crazy about her. Warmth spread through Ivy at Finn's words. She studied her hands, a smile tugging at her lips. "He's pretty tough to resist when he sets his mind to something."

"Hey, Finn, have you seen—oh, sorry." Garrett

rounded the corner and came to an abrupt halt in the doorway of the breakfast room when he spied Ivy sitting at the table with Finn. He stared at her for a full two seconds, his face expressing surprise, pleasure and something that looked suspiciously like regret, before he composed his features into an impassive mask. "I didn't mean to interrupt."

"No, you're not interrupting," Finn assured him. "Ivy and I were just finishing our discussion. Speaking of which…"

Finn's eyes shifted beyond Garrett to the lobby, where two women walked slowly toward them. One was older, and limped slightly with each step. She leaned on the arm of a younger, strikingly attractive brunette.

"Garrett!" the younger woman exclaimed upon seeing him standing in the doorway. "There you are. I've been looking everywhere for you!"

Ivy felt her insides shrivel as the younger woman released her companion's arm and strode across the space separating her from Garrett. She wore a simple white tank top and a pair of figure-hugging jeans, and had paired them with heeled sandals that lent additional height to her willowy frame. Even so, Garrett topped her by a good six inches. He turned in surprise as she called his name, and just barely managed to catch her before she launched herself into his arms.

"Hey," he said, laughing in pleasure as he closed his arms around her. "I didn't know you'd be here. This is wonderful!"

Ivy felt ill. Obviously, this was Helena Vanderveer, and she could understand why he'd been so attracted to her. The woman was gorgeous, and her entire body exuded a passionate energy. As she hugged Garrett, there was no mistaking the emotion on her face. She loved him.

When Garrett finally set her away, she grabbed his arm with excitement. "Oh, you'll never guess who was on the connecting flight from Mexico City with me! Wait till you see!"

Garrett glanced once at Ivy, who sat rigidly in her chair, unable to move. Beneath his tan, he was ashen. Every cell in her body wanted to leap up and dash out of the room before she was forced to witness any more of their reunion. Instead, she sat there with a phony smile pasted on her face, pretending interest, while her chest constricted with her every breath.

Now the older woman stepped forward. Despite her limp, she was sturdy, with short graying hair, a friendly face and a wholesome appearance. Her eyes were bright with pleasure as she took Garrett's hand between both of hers and smiled up at him.

Was it Garrett's mother? Ivy glanced uncertainly at Finn, who had risen to his feet with a satisfied smile. For Ivy, it was about as much as she could stomach. Standing up, she clutched her bag and glanced apologetically at Finn.

"I'm sorry. I really need to head over to makeup—"

"No, just wait a moment," Finn said, forestalling her with a raised hand. "I want you to meet Helena."

It was the absolute last thing Ivy wanted. Short of being rude, however, she had no choice but to stand beside him and behold the drama before her with a sinking heart.

The older woman was squeezing Garrett's hand and nodding in approval as her eyes traveled over him. "You look very different zan zee last time I saw you," she said in a heavily accented voice. "You probably do not remember me. You voor badly injured."

To Ivy's astonishment, Garrett lifted the woman's hand to his lips. "Ma'am," he said, his voice rough, "I could never forget my guardian angel." The woman laughed in delight, and Garrett released her hand to lean down and embrace her. "I can never thank you enough for what you did for me."

"Oh, pleeze," she said, patting his back before he released her. "To see you in such good health is tanks enuff. I heard that you voor in Mexico, and decided I must see you for myself before I return to Amsterdam."

Ivy couldn't prevent the small gasp of dismay that escaped her lips, even as her mind reeled with shock. This was Helena Vanderveer! A woman old enough to be Garrett's mother; a woman Garrett apparently had little recollection of due to his extensive injuries.

Recalling the multiple scars on his body, Ivy almost groaned at her own gullibility. It was so obvious that he wouldn't have been in any shape for a seduction. How could she have fallen for such a patent impossibility?

Because she, herself, had wanted him.

Ivy ignored the tiny voice. It didn't matter whether she'd wanted him or not—what he'd done was wrong.

"I heard you were ill," Garrett was saying.

Helena waved dismissively. "Just my pesky hip. My doctors vill giff me a new one."

They stood smiling at each other for a moment, until the younger woman cleared her throat in a meaningful way. Garrett started and his gaze snapped to Ivy. To her amazement, two ruddy patches rode high on his cheekbones.

"Ivy James," Finn said, drawing her forward, "I'd like you to meet my wife, Savannah."

"I'm Finn's wife and Garrett's sister," the woman said, slanting an affectionate glance toward Garrett.

Ivy stared at the other woman as they shook hands. Now that she knew the truth, the strong family resemblance was hard to miss. Suddenly, she understood the expression she'd seen on Savannah's face as she'd hugged Garrett. Not that of an adoring lover, but one of an adoring *sister*.

"It's wonderful to finally meet you," Savannah said with a warm smile. "I've seen all your movies." Her glance slid back to Garrett and a mischievous grin curved her mouth. "At least a hundred times."

"Savannah," Garrett warned in a low voice.

"And this amazing lady," Finn continued, putting an arm around the older woman's shoulders, "is the real-life inspiration for your character, Helena Vanderveer."

Helena stepped forward and, just as she had done with Garrett, took Ivy's hand between both of her own. "Hello, my dear," she said, smiling into Ivy's eyes. "I tink dat maybe you did not know I vass an old vooman."

Ivy struggled to contain her rioting emotions—confusion, embarrassment, complete and overwhelming relief and, beneath that, a growing indignation.

Garrett had completely lied to her. Again.

The first time had been by omission, in not telling her he'd played a vital part in getting her cast for the role of Helena Vanderveer by bringing Ivy to Finn's attention. But this...this had been a deliberate and outright fabrication about his relationship with the missionary for the sole purpose of getting her to sleep with him.

"Ah, no," she said with a swift, self-conscious smile. "I didn't realize that the real Helena wasn't—that she was—that you were—" Ivy was perilously close to tears.

"It's my fault," Garrett interjected. "I told her that every aspect of the script was based on true events. She had no reason not to believe me."

But I did believe you.

Ivy didn't miss how Savannah's eyes widened at her brother's admission, before she rolled them in exasperation. Ivy didn't trust herself to look at Garrett. She was afraid if she did, she would crumble. She would break down and rail at him for deceiving her in such an underhanded way, and then sob her relief that he hadn't been in love with the Dutch missionary.

She needed to get out of there before she said or did something she'd regret.

"You know what?" She smiled brightly at them. "It's fine. Really. Garrett was just trying to help me get into character, at least as it was depicted in the script, and I'm grateful to him for that." She leaned forward and gave Helena a brief hug. "I'm so happy for the opportunity to meet you." Her voice dropped to a whisper, meant for Helena's ears only. "And thank you, from the bottom of my heart, for saving him."

Helena squeezed Ivy's shoulders. "I tink he is a good man. If I had your yout and beauty, I vood not let him get avay."

Ivy nodded and, straightening, pretended to rummage through her bag. "I, um, have to get over to hair and makeup," she said. "If you'll excuse me."

Without looking at any of them, she hurried from the room, making a beeline for the exit. She was halfway across the courtyard, when she heard his voice behind her.

"Ivy, wait." His tone was insistent. "Ivy, *damn it,* will you wait?"

She broke into a trot, aware he'd have difficulty keeping up with her. If she wanted to, she could completely outrun him. She made it just beyond the courtyard, to the pathway that led down to his *casita,* before she stopped, chest heaving. He was on her less than a second later, stopping a foot away.

"Ivy," he said, extending his hands toward her. "I'm sorry, sweetheart. I wanted to tell you—I really did. But—"

"But what? You wanted to sleep with me more than you wanted to tell me the truth?"

She'd never seen such an expression on Garrett's face; it was both anguished and desperate. He looked as miserable as she felt. Up close to him now, she could see his eyes were bloodshot, as if he hadn't slept, and his face was covered with a day's growth of whiskers. Even his hair looked as though he'd spent the past several hours raking his fingers through it.

"I never intended to deceive you—I want you to believe that." His voice was earnest. "But that first day, when you asked me if the scenes with Helena were based on reality…" He ran a hand through his hair. "I never thought the deception would go as far as it did. I figured that at some point, either in your discussions with Finn, or with the other cast members, you'd realize that not only was Helena old enough to be my mother, but that I was too badly injured to even know what was happening during those days at the mission. Forgive me. Please."

Ivy shook her head in bemusement. "Why did you let me go on and on, asking you to give me *pointers,* like some kind of idiot?"

She didn't protest when he took her face between his

big hands. His eyes were heated and tender as they traveled over her features. "Don't you know?"

Ivy felt her chest constrict, and her voice croaked when she spoke. "Tell me."

"I love you. I have since the first moment I saw you in that hospital, when all I wanted to do was pull you into my arms and comfort you." He smiled crookedly. "Instead, all I could do was watch you leave."

Ivy searched his eyes, seeing the truth in their light brown depths. "But you lied to me."

Garrett groaned. "Don't think it didn't keep me up at night, because it did. I'm not proud of myself, but put yourself in my place. The woman of my dreams—the one woman in the world I'm absolutely nuts about and I'd do anything for—asks me to re-create a love scene with her, believing it will help her improve her acting skills." His thumbs smoothed over her cheeks and he looked directly into her eyes. "What was I supposed to do? Tell you the truth—that there was no love affair—and let you go into the reshoot with no idea how to make it work? Or let you go to Terrell to practice the scenes?" He shook his head. "No way."

Ivy's heart began to knock hard against her ribs, and of their own volition, her hands came up to cover his. "So you—you used me." Even to her own ears, her words lacked conviction.

"No, baby. Never." His eyes searched hers. "I *loved* you."

"But how?"

Garrett laughed softly. "How could I love you? It's the easiest thing in the world."

Ivy closed her eyes, unwilling to let herself be drawn into the irresistible promise she saw shimmering in his eyes. "How do I know your love is real? How do I know it will last beyond filming? That once we're back to the real world, with you at Fort Bragg and me in New York, it won't just end?"

She didn't resist when he gave a heartfelt groan and hauled her into his arms. "You have to trust me on this, sweetheart. I'm not going anywhere. If New York is where you want to be, then we'll make it work, I swear. North Carolina isn't all that far from the Big Apple. I could probably catch an early flight every morning and be at Fort Bragg in time for role call."

Ivy tilted her head back to stare at him. "Are you serious?"

"Absolutely."

She started to smile. She couldn't help herself.

"What?" He frowned down at her. "You don't believe me?"

Ivy shook her head in confusion. "I don't know what to believe. This is all so…crazy."

"It might seem like that, but I have never been more serious about anything in my entire life. I was half in love with you before I ever met you, but I realize now that was the equivalent of an adolescent crush." He brushed a loose tendril of hair back from her forehead. "What I feel for you—it defies words. The only thing I do know is that it's *real.*"

Ivy searched his eyes, and found the truth reflected there. "I knew there was something familiar about you the first time we met, but I couldn't put my finger on it. It was like a—a connection of some kind." She managed a weak smile. "I was so attracted to you that first day, by the pool, when I was wearing those awful clothes."

Garrett smiled. "You looked amazing."

"I looked terrible. Then, later that night…" She

stopped and bit her lip, remembering how much she'd wanted him.

"I wanted you, too," he said, reading her thoughts. "I still do. I always will. That won't ever stop."

"Garrett…" The love in his eyes robbed her of breath.

He cupped her face and tilted it up, his lips almost touching hers. "So the only question is…do you forgive me? Do you love me? Can we try to make this work?"

Ivy's breath caught in her throat, and she smiled against his mouth. "Yes," she breathed. "Yes. And yes."

Epilogue

One Year Later

THE SLEEK BLACK LIMOUSINE drew to a halt in front of Grauman's Chinese Theatre on Hollywood Boulevard. Ivy peered out the tinted glass windows at the towering coral-red columns that supported the traditional Chinese pagoda-style architecture, and at the massive stone-carved dragon that twisted over the entrance. A red carpet had been rolled across the ground from the curb where the limousine was parked to the entry itself. Red velvet roping cordoned off the walkway from the throngs of paparazzi and eager fans who lined the sidewalks on either side, clamoring for a view of the celebrities as they arrived.

Ivy stared at the brilliantly lit marquee on either side of the entrance. There, in enormous letters, were the words *World Premiere…Eye of the Hunter.* Beneath the name of the film, were the names *Eric Terrell* and *Ivy James,* in brilliant neon lights.

A hand descended warmly on her bare shoulder, caressing her skin. "You did it, sweetheart. They say this film is going to earn you an Academy Award nomination."

Ivy turned in the seat toward Garrett. He was gorgeous in a tailored suit, and although she hadn't quite gotten used to his newly cropped hair, she silently acknowledged that it gave him a whole new appeal. He looked like every woman's fantasy.

"I can hardly believe it." She smiled and leaned across to give him a lingering kiss. "It's like a dream come true. And I'm not just talking about the films."

She was talking about him, and how he'd kept his promise to make their relationship work. He had a home in North Carolina, not far from Fort Bragg, and she had a small apartment in New York City. Despite a some-times hectic filming schedule, they'd resolved never to be apart for more than three nights. So far, they were succeeding.

"You'd better get used to this," Garrett murmured against her lips, "since I'd be willing to bet the last two films you made are going to do as well, if not better, than this one."

The door to the limousine opened. Ivy climbed out and took Garrett's hand, nearly blinded by the bright flashes of the cameras.

Reporters shouted questions. "Ms. James," called one woman, "I see you're here tonight with the man who inspired this movie."

"Yes," Ivy said, smiling and twining her fingers with Garrett's. "This is Garrett Stokes, the real-life hero of this amazing story."

"Is it true that you and Mr. Stokes are engaged to be married?"

"It's true," Garrett said with a smile, bringing Ivy's hand to his lips.

They were barraged with more questions as they made their way slowly toward the entrance to the theater.

"What about your leading man, Ms. James? He

hasn't made an appearance yet tonight. Does he plan to attend the premiere?"

Ivy drew Garrett to a stop on the red carpet. "Actually," she said, "my leading man is right here." She looked into Garrett's eyes. "This is my leading man, now and forever."

And as the cameras continued to flash around them, they gave their onlookers a kiss worthy of an Academy Award.

* * * * *

Turn the page for a sneak preview of
AFTERSHOCK, *a new anthology*
featuring New York Times *bestselling author*
Sharon Sala.

Available October 2008.

n o c t u r n e ™

Dramatic and sensual tales of paranormal romance.

Chapter 1

October
New York City

Nicole Masters was sitting cross-legged on her sofa while a cold autumn rain peppered the windows of her fourth-floor apartment. She was poking at the ice cream in her bowl and trying not to be in a mood.

Six weeks ago, a simple trip to her neighborhood pharmacy had turned into a nightmare. She'd walked into the middle of a robbery. She never even saw the man who shot her in the head and left her for dead. She'd survived, but some of her senses had not. She was dealing with short-term memory loss and a tendency to stagger. Even though she'd been told the problems were most likely temporary, she waged a daily battle with depression.

Her parents had been killed in a car wreck when she was twenty-one. And except for a few friends—and most recently her boyfriend, Dominic Tucci, who lived in the apartment right above hers—she was alone. Her doctor kept reminding her that she should be grateful to be alive, and on one level she knew he was right. But he wasn't living in her shoes.

If she'd been anywhere else but at that pharmacy when the robbery happened, she wouldn't have died twice on the way to the hospital. Instead of being grateful that she'd survived, she couldn't stop thinking of what she'd lost.

But that wasn't the end of her troubles. On top of everything else, something strange was happening inside her head. She'd begun to hear odd things: sounds, not voices—at least, she didn't think it was voices. It was more like the distant noise of rapids—a rush of wind and water inside her head that, when it came, blocked out everything around her. It didn't happen often, but when it did, it was frightening, and it was driving her crazy.

The blank moments, which is what she called them, even had a rhythm. First there came that sound, then a cold sweat, then panic with no reason. Part of her feared it was the beginning of an emotional breakdown. And part of her feared it wasn't—that it was going to turn out to be a permanent souvenir of her resurrection.

Frustrated with herself and the situation as it stood, she upped the sound on the TV remote. But instead of *Wheel of Fortune,* an announcer broke in with a special bulletin.

"This just in. Police are on the scene of a kidnapping that occurred only hours ago at The Dakota. Molly Dane, the six-year-old daughter of one of Hollywood's blockbuster stars, Lyla Dane, was taken by force from the family apartment. At this time they have yet to receive a ransom demand. The housekeeper was seriously injured during the abduction, and is, at the present time, in surgery. Police are hoping to be able to talk to her once she regains consciousness. In the meantime, we are going now to a press conference with Lyla Dane."

Horrified, Nicole stilled as the cameras went live to where the actress was speaking before a bank of microphones. The shock and terror in Lyla Dane's voice were physically painful to watch. But even though Nicole kept upping the volume, the sound continued to fade.

Just when she was beginning to think something was wrong with her set, the broadcast suddenly switched from the Dane press conference to what appeared to be footage of the kidnapping, beginning with footage from inside the apartment.

When the front door suddenly flew back against the wall and four men rushed in, Nicole gasped. Horrified, she quickly realized that this must have been caught on a security camera inside the Dane apartment.

As Nicole continued to watch, a small Asian woman, who she guessed was the maid, rushed forward in an effort to keep them out. When one of the men hit her in the face with his gun, Nicole moaned. The violence was too reminiscent of what she'd lived through. Sick to her stomach, she fisted her hands against her belly, wishing it was over, but unable to tear her gaze away.

When the maid dropped to the carpet, the same man followed with a vicious kick to the little woman's midsection that lifted her off the floor.

"Oh, my God," Nicole said. When blood began to pool beneath the maid's head, she started to cry.

As the tape played on, the four men split up in

different directions. The camera caught one running down a long marble hallway, then disappearing into a room. Moments later he reappeared, carrying a little girl, who Nicole assumed was Molly Dane. The child was wearing a pair of red pants and a white turtleneck sweater, and her hair was partially blocking her abductor's face as he carried her down the hall. She was kicking and screaming in his arms, and when he slapped her, it elicited an agonized scream that brought the other three running. Nicole watched in horror as one of them ran up and put his hand over Molly's face. Seconds later, she went limp.

One moment they were in the foyer, then they were gone.

Nicole jumped to her feet, then staggered drunkenly. The bowl of ice cream she'd absentmindedly placed in her lap shattered at her feet, splattering glass and melting ice cream everywhere.

The picture on the screen abruptly switched from the kidnapping to what Nicole assumed was a rerun of Lyla Dane's plea for her daughter's safe return, but she was numb.

Before she could think what to do next, the doorbell rang. Startled by the unexpected sound, she shakily swiped at the tears and took a step forward. She didn't feel the glass shards piercing her feet until she took the second step. At that point, sharp pains shot through her foot. She gasped, then looked down in confusion. Her legs looked as if she'd been running through mud, and she was standing in broken glass and ice cream, while a thin ribbon of blood seepesd out from beneath her toes.

"Oh, no," Nicole mumbled, then stifled a second moan of pain.

The doorbell rang again. She shivered, then clutched her head in confusion.

"Just a minute!" she yelled, then tried to sidestep the rest of the debris as she hobbled to the door.

When she looked through the peephole in the door, she didn't know whether to be relieved or regretful.

It was Dominic, and as usual, she was a mess.

Nicole smiled a little self-consciously as she opened the door to let him in. "I just don't know what's happening to me. I think I'm losing my mind."

"Hey, don't talk about my woman like that."

Nicole rode the surge of delight his words brought. "So I'm still your woman?"

Dominic lowered his head.

Their lips met.

The kiss proceeded.

Slowly.

Thoroughly.

* * * * *

Be sure to look for the **AFTERSHOCK** *anthology next month, as well as other exciting paranormal stories from Silhouette Nocturne. Available in October wherever books are sold.*

nocturne™

NEW YORK TIMES BESTSELLING AUTHOR

SHARON SALA

JANIS REAMES HUDSON
DEBRA COWAN

AFTERSHOCK

Three women are brought to the brink of death...
only to discover the aftershock of their trauma has
left them with unexpected and unwelcome gifts of
paranormal powers. Now each woman must learn to
accept her newfound abilities while fighting for life,
love and second chances....

Available October wherever books are sold.

www.eHarlequin.com
www.paranormalromanceblog.wordpress.com   SN61796

REQUEST YOUR FREE BOOKS!

2 FREE NOVELS PLUS 2 FREE GIFTS!

HARLEQUIN®

Blaze™

Red-hot reads!

Harlequin® Historical
Historical Romantic Adventure!

HALLOWE'EN HUSBANDS

With three fantastic stories by

Lisa Plumley
Denise Lynn
Christine Merrill

Don't miss these unforgettable
stories about three women who
experience the mysterious
happenings of Allhallows Eve
and come to discover that finding
true love on this eerie day is not
so scary after all.

Look for
HALLOWE'EN HUSBANDS

Available October
wherever books are sold.

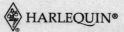

HARLEQUIN®

Blaze™

COMING NEXT MONTH

#423 LETHAL EXPOSURE Lori Wilde
Perfect Anatomy, Bk. 3

Wanting to expand her sexual IQ, Julie DeMarco selects Sebastian Black—hotshot PR exec—to participate in a no-strings fling. The playboy should be an easygoing love-'em-and-leave-'em type, but what if there's more to the man than just his good looks?

#424 MS. MATCH Jo Leigh
The Wrong Bed

Oops! It's the wrong sister! Paul Bennet agrees to take plain Jane Gwen Christopher on a charity date only to score points with her gorgeous sister. So what is he thinking when he wakes up beside Gwen the very next morning?

#425 AMOROUS LIAISONS Sarah Mayberry
Lust in Translation

Max Laurent thought he was over his attraction to Maddy Green. But when she shows up on the doorstep of his Paris flat, it turns out the lust never went away. He's determined to stay silent so as not to ruin their friendship—until the night she seduces him, that is.

#426 GOOD TO THE LAST BITE Crystal Green

Vampire Edward Marburn has only one goal left—to take vengeance on Gisele, the female vamp who'd stolen his humanity. Before long, Edward has Gisele right where he wants her. And he learns that the joys of sexual revenge can last an eternity....

#427 HER SECRET TREASURE Cindi Myers

Adam Carroway never thought he'd agree to work with Sandra Newman. Hit the sheets with her...absolutely. But work together? Still, his expedition needs the publicity her TV show will bring. Besides, what could be sexier than working out their differences in bed?

#428 WATCH AND LEARN Stephanie Bond
Sex for Beginners, Bk. 1

When recently divorced Gemma Jacobs receives a letter she'd written to herself ten years ago in college, she never guesses the contents will inspire her to take charge of her sexuality, to unleash her forbidden exhibitionist tendencies...and to seduce her totally hot, voyeuristic new neighbor....